For Vicky Kenmay.
We all miss you, darlin'.

Chapter 1

One Saturday morning, not very long ago, I dropped dead and turned into a duppy.

Some finicky members of the book-buying public will no doubt challenge this opening. (I welcome this opposition.)

They will gripe, as a friend of mine did when I showed him this first page, "Baps, you expect me to pay hard-earned money for a book whose writer dead in de opening sentence? If de writer dead in the beginning, who write the book? Duppy?"

Being dead is most definitely an impediment to writing a book—under ordinary circumstances. Proof that death is a challenging obstacle to a literary career is to be found in the fact that, to the best of my knowledge, there is not a single case of a Jamaican duppy ever publishing a book on the island. Not one.

Moreover, as everyone knows, the common pastime of Jamaican duppy—to romp on the naked bellies of sleeping church sisters—is an entirely frivolous one that requires no formal schooling, literacy, or intellectual skills. Indeed, it is widely believed, and I myself believe it, that Jamaican duppy is illiterate, no free places in the schools ever having been set aside by successive governments for education of the substantial duppy population known to roam the island.

The pertinent point is, if the writer is dead in sentence one and duppy is an ignoramus who can't even recite his *ABC*'s, how came this book to be written?

All these questions, and sundry others, will be fully addressed and answered in the coming pages.

For now, I beg the reader just to grant me this: One Saturday morning, not very long ago, I did drop dead. And I definitely turned into a duppy.

My name is Taddeus Augustus Baps. I was born in Kingston, the only child of a decent working-class family. At the time of my death I owned three country shops, although strictly speaking I had been trained to be a teacher and had taught in the secondary schools for some ten years until dire poverty compelled me to take up a more commercial livelihood.

I started out small, buying my first country shop from a retired gentleman who was migrating to Canada to join his grown children. A few years later I expanded to a second shop and then to a third.

On the morning of my death, I had woken early and shuffled through the dawn dimness cobwebbing the hallways of my Kingston house, intending to go over my accounts.

I sat on a hassock in the drawing room and did the books while the usual nightly gabble of dog bark over the neighbourhood was quieting down along with the throbbing of distant sound systems. Except for the scratching of my pencil and the sounds of a rooster gargling dew in the dawn light, the morning was peaceful.

I was carefully writing down a naught when I felt a vicious tearing inside my chest like a crab had squeezed behind my breastbone and was ripping my heart out with its claws. My breath was abruptly stopped up. I scratched at my chest and moaned with a wicked pain.

Before I could even bawl out a common Jamaican shopkeeping phrase such as, "Stop, thief!" I toppled off

2

my chair and hit the floor with a loud crash that rattled my house down to its very foundations.

I was only forty-seven years old.

I was also stone dead.

But I did not immediately realise that I was dead.

That is the strange thing about turning duppy: at first you don't know it. Your duppy floats out of your dead body and you look around and think, "Boy, dis is funny! I slip and drop on de ground, but I feel better now!"

So it was with me. Indeed, when my duppy got up off the floor, I felt a little giddy but thought that I was still in the land of the living.

I looked around the room and tried to grasp what was happening when I noticed that the exercise book in which I kept my accounts had flown out of my hands and landed in a corner and the pencil had dropped beside the hassock and rolled under the chair.

As I am a man who hates untidiness, I got down on my hands and knees to pick up the exercise book and discovered, to my shock, that I couldn't grab hold of it, that my hands suddenly seemed made of wisps. Every time I grabbed at the book, it slipped through the mist of my fingers.

Next I tried picking up the pencil and found that my fingers passed right through the shaft. Perplexed, I thought to call Mabel, my new maid, and beg her boil a cup of strong breakfast tea to clear my head.

I had just opened my mouth to bawl out Mabel's name when I glimpsed something funny in my drawing room. I couldn't tell what it was at first because of the fuzzy morning light, but as I drew closer, I saw that it was the body of a heavy-set black man lying crumpled on the floor.

What was this? I indignantly asked myself. Had some ole negar come and dead in my drawing room at this early hour without asking permission?

I was about to kick the brute and tell him to get up and go dead on government road when I realised—to my horror—that the ole negar dead on the floor was none other than me, Taddeus Baps.

I started one unearthly piece of wailing. I bawled out loud: "De ole negar dead on de floor is me! Lawd, Jesus, I dead and turn duppy! And I wasn't even sick! Now me dead!"

Then I flew into a temper, for I am not a man who yields lightly to life's obstacles.

Who said I should dead now? I asked myself angrily. I was only forty-seven years old! I certainly wasn't going to dead without a fight!

Getting down on my knees, I tried to ram my duppy body back inside my carcass.

But my own earthly body had become a wall that my duppy couldn't penetrate. My duppy hand bounced off the fleshy limb. Duppy foot wouldn't slide into real foot. Trying to stuff my duppy head back inside my skull was like bucking against a rusty engine block.

I stood up and started my bawling all over again. I cussed bad word and popped wicked oaths and swore that I wasn't leaving my body behind for worms to eat.

But all my wailing and cussing didn't make the slightest difference.

As you will find out for yourself one day, once your time has come to dead and turn duppy, no amount of bawling can bring you back.

And I had unquestionably turned duppy.

Chapter 2

In the dimness of the Kingston dawn, I was standing confused in my sparsely furnished drawing room trying to decide what to do now that I was a duppy instead of an enumerated voter when I heard a scuffling noise coming from the hallway and my maid, Mabel, calling, "Mr. Baps! Mr. Baps!"

"Help, Mabel!" I yelled. "You poor employer dead and turn duppy!"

I cocked my ear to listen for an answer but heard only the shrill thread of a rooster's crowing unreeling in the blurry light.

A few seconds later Mabel renewed her bleating. She shuffled into the doorway, poked her head cautiously around the doorjamb, and squinted into the dim room.

She stared, hesitated, and without even drawing closer, blasted out a howl, "Mr. Baps dead! Mr. Baps dead!"

I yelled back, "Yes! And dead because of you! If I told you once I told you a hundred times, don't cook wid de blessed coconut oil dat so full of cholesterol! But you wouldn't listen! And now because you so hard-o'-hearing, you bad oil kill me off in me own drawing room!"

I was going to add that perhaps the whole thing was a mistake, a dreadful nightmare, but I kept this encouraging thought to myself because I have always frowned on open familiarity between employer and domestic unless the domestic's drawers were down and she was wriggling underneath her employer, in which case some familiarity and sweetmouthing were clearly warranted.

5

Before I could say another word, however, Mabel had scampered screaming down the hallway, her frantic footsteps rumbling through the wooden house, making the walls tremble.

She returned a few minutes later dragging Hector, the old gardener, into the room, and the two of them approached my dead body cautiously on tiptoe. The gardener bent over and felt for a pulse while Mabel tried vainly to pry open my closed eyelid with a greasy thumb.

"What happen?" she asked in a quaking voice, kneeling beside my body.

"Mr. Baps dead, is what happen," the gardener replied sourly, lumbering to his feet with much popping of old bone.

"Listen to me!" I urged, trying my best to stay calm. "I can still see and hear you, so it's not as bad as it looks. Can you hear me? How I look? Do I look dead? I don't feel dead! I just outta me body! Odderwise, I feel strong. How I look?"

It was obvious that they could neither see nor hear my duppy self, for the two of them ignored my questions and just stood there staring down at my dead body.

Mabel's face hardened like quarry rockstone. "So because Mr. Baps decide to dead now, I must go look for a new job? You think work easy to find?"

"Oh, no," the gardener said amiably. "But Mr. Baps clearly dead. And if you think him was tight with money when him was living, now dat him dead you really going see tight."

"I wasn't dat tight! Shame on you, talking so 'bout you employer who just dead!"

They moped around in the drawing room staring glumly at my dead body as if uncertain about what to do next.

"Him pay you for de week before him dead?" Mabel asked.

"No," the gardener replied sullenly.

"So check him wallet! If de police find any money on him, you know dem bound to thief it."

The gardener eagerly obeyed and found my wallet stuffed full of money, for I had not yet made the weekly bank lodgement.

He counted out his week's wages and gave Mabel her own and was about to return the wallet when she asked crossly whether he thought it was right for an employer to dead without giving staff proper notice.

"Notice?" the gardener sniffed legalistically, as a thiefing gleam spread across his wrinkled face. "No, dat definitely not right, for de law say two weeks' notice always must give. No exception."

"You think man dead like bus run?" I quarrelled with them. "If I had known I was going to drop dead, I would have gladly given de proper notice and saved two weeks' wages. But how you expect me to know?"

This logical point, however, made no impression whatsoever on the two hardened criminals, who gladly pocketed another helping of my hard-earned money with hoggish snorts of pleasure.

The gardener knelt down and was again about to return my wallet to my back pocket when Mabel scowled and rapped him sharply on the shoulder.

"What about Christmas bonus? Is our fault dat Mr. Baps dead out of season?"

"No," the gardener said slowly, rubbing his chin as if in deep thought, "clearly is not our fault. I never tell him to dead at dis special time. You tell him to dead?"

"Me? No, sah!"

"So him just wilfully make up him mind to dead on him own?"

"Exactly! So why we should lose we rightful bonus just because him decide him mind to drop dead before Christmas?"

This was too much. I shrieked, "I never pay a Christmas bonus in me life! Don't make me pay one now dat I dead!"

Nevertheless, Christmas bonus money drained out of my wallet into their pockets and no matter how I grabbed at this one and kicked at that, I was powerless to prevent this unlawful transfer of funds. I yelled and screamed and cussed bad words and made a lot of duppy noise but it did no good.

In addition to bonuses for Christmas, Boxing Day, and Easter, the two wretches also found excuse to thief birthday and Leap Year money (I laughed with scorn at the ignorant brutes who didn't even know that this wasn't a Leap Year!), and when they finally returned my wallet to my back pocket, it was as flabby and limp as a fat fish after gutting.

Whistling, the gardener strolled down the hall to call the police while Mabel settled into an easy chair, cocked up her bare foot on my head, and picked at knuckle skin like she was born mistress of the house.

"Lawd God," my duppy moaned, "I just dead and already ole negar using me head as dem footstool. What further tribulation can dis terrible day bring, eh?"

Chapter 3

In my youth I was a worthless, good-for-nothing, undisciplined idler. And I might have stayed that way, too, except for a life-changing sermon I heard one Sunday morning on the radio.

It was given by an evangelist who griped that people relied too much on the influence of preachers when what they really needed to better their lives was daily self-preaching. For what was wrong with a sinner preaching to himself?—the evangelist asked. Who better understood a dirty lowdown sinner than the dirty lowdown sinner himself? Who knew more about nasty, stinking sin than a nasty, stinking, sinning wretch?

This message made so much sense to me that from that day on I started practising a stern treatment of self-preaching. And I preached at myself so often that one morning when I was in my late thirties, I awoke convinced that a parson had set up manse and pulpit inside my head.

So on the morning of my death, after the initial shock had passed and I was beginning to feel sorry for myself, I counteracted my downheartedness with this sermon.

"Baps, you lazy, good-for-nothing brute! Woe unto you! Stop you snivelling! You dead and gone! You maid and garden boy thief out de weekly lodgement money! You turn dirty duppy, Baps!"

After this spontaneous outburst of devout feeling from my indoor parson, I thought to look at the positive side of things and take a moment to count my blessings as a duppy.

It struck me at once that from now on I could observe all crooked money-changing at the bank. I could overhear scandal and rumour, eavesdrop on backbiting and tale-telling as well as witness all unlawful maid grinding taking place between employer and domestic in the corporate area. I could walk through brick, concrete block, wattle and daub, or wooden wall to personally see which government minister had his hand in the cash pan.

To prove that all this was so, I waded through the outside wall and stepped into the unkempt side yard. After that, I sifted back through the solid wall and ended up again in my own drawing room where Mabel still slouched in my favourite chair, picking at her knuckles, her bare foot cocked atop my head.

Suddenly I suffered temptation: if my hand could pass through a wall, couldn't it also pass through frock and drawers? Indeed, as I scrutinised the luscious shape of Mabel draped across the chair, it occurred to me that the one benefit of being a duppy was that there wasn't a woman in the world I couldn't feel up from now on without fear of scandal and prosecution.

To test this newfound duppy power, I ploughed my hand deep into Mabel's crotch. My duppy fingers glided through dress and drawers and came out wriggling giddily on the other side of her fatty rump.

But her crotch had no feeling to my touch; there was no wholesome grit to the pubic hair, and the pumpum felt empty and wishy-washy like idle land.

Although I was disappointed with the results, I remembered that it was church sisters who were always complaining about duppy riding them at night. Obviously, if Mabel had been a church sister instead of a stinking thief, things might have turned out differently. What I needed to find was a sleeping church sister I could take on a test ride.

I was pondering this hopeful thought when there was suddenly a sharp rap on the front door. Mabel didn't move a muscle but continued to peer into space like an old woman listening to her own growling belly. The knocking grew louder.

"Who's it?" I bellowed and into the room through the closed door stepped a boy named Hopeton who used to live and work in the neighbourhood.

For a moment I couldn't believe my eyes.

The boy had been dead for years and yet here he was standing before me as solid as a ripe breadfruit. I blinked and squinted and my mouth dropped open. "Hopeton?" I blurted, gaping at him. "Is you dat?"

"Yes, sah," he grinned.

"But don't Mr. Byles shoot you dead five years ago when you try to break his house?"

"Yes, sah. Kill me stone dead."

"So what you doing here, man?"

"I come to escort you across, Mr. Baps," he said, waving duppy finger in my face.

"Kiss my backside!" I blurted.

Before the boy could take another step, I raced down the hallway, flew through the side wall and out into the backyard where I scurried high up into a mango tree and crouched behind a thick clump of leaves.

I was ducking behind the shiny leaves high up in the crown of the mango tree when I heard Hopeton scouring the backyard and bawling out my name.

"Mr. Baps!" he was hollering. "Oyea! Mr. Baps!"

He bawled some more and when I finally got enough nerve to timidly peek out I saw that he was standing at the root of the tree, squinting up at me with his arms on his hips, looking peevish in the bad light.

"Hopeton!" I cried, ducking behind my leafy cover. "I wasn't feeling up Mabel! I didn't even know my hand had passed through her pumpum and out her batty! I not used to duppy finger!"

"Mr. Baps, come down, sah! I don't business who you feel up."

"I wasn't going to ride no church sister, either! It was just an idle thought! You can't carry a Jamaican to hell just for thinking! Dis is not Castro's Cuba! Socialism days done! All I did is feel up one thiefing maid!"

"Mr. Baps," Hopeton chuckled after a long crack of silence, "dere is no hell, sah! Dere is only one place, and dat is where I come to carry you."

I didn't believe him—at least not at first. I stayed up in the tree while he and I bellowed back and forth between tree-top and root-bottom, but after plenty argument I became convinced that he was telling the truth and clambered down the gnarled trunk to stand beside him.

He started walking back towards the house, looking over his shoulder to see if I was following.

Dawn had broken over Kingston and a pulpy morning glow, still damp with the lingering coolness of night, was settling over the neighbourhood.

I must admit that I was still suspicious, although I said nothing and quietly trailed him down the bushy side yard.

Even though I was not a religious man, I had never imagined that when I died I would be escorted to heaven by a shot thief. I don't want to sound stuck-up but I just thought I deserved a better class duppy guide—a chartered accountant, a barrister, or some other fully qualified professional. I could have even been content with a registered nurse or a university trained teacher. But if I had to settle for an uneducated duppy guide, then I thought I at least deserved better than one who had departed earth via gunshot administered during the felonious act of house-breaking.

So I felt slighted and had hurt feelings that I counted so little with Almighty God.

As we made our way out from the backyard and into the house, my brain kept harping morbidly on what Hopeton had said about there being no hell.

How could there be no hell? And if there really was no hell, what happened to gunmen when they died? Must decent people be chuck-up in heaven cheek-to-cheek with the ruthless criminal element? Must I spend eternity croaking "Hosanna" in a choir with a butu rabble I would kick off my doorstep?

As we glided through the wall of my former house and into the drawing room, I was going to put some arguments to Hopeton when my chain of thought was interrupted by the sight of two burly policemen kneeling down over my dead body and in the middle of a heated argument with the maid and the gardener.

One policeman was waving my empty wallet about, showing that it contained only a twenty-dollar bill and bellowing that nobody in Jamaica dropped dead with only twenty dollars in his possession, that someone had thiefed government evidence. The gardener was blubbering that he personally knew plenty man who had dropped dead with only a dollar on them, at which allegation the other policeman took out a notepad and sarcastically asked for the names of these alleged deceased paupers.

"Names, sah?" the gardener stammered. "Me no remember exact name, sah. But me know dat man dead all de time in Jamaica without money in him pocket."

"Somebody thief dis man money," the other policeman growled, standing up and peering hard at the gardener and the maid. "Either dat, or him not really dead."

And to demonstrate that I was really dead, the policeman rocked my body with a wicked kick, which brought a thunderous howl of grief from Mabel.

"Don't kick Mr. Baps!" she shrieked, jumping between my dead body and the policeman's foot, water spurting from her eyes. "Him was de most blessed man dat ever walk dis earth. Him give 'way him every penny him have to de poor. Nobody ever beg him anything dat him wouldn't give. Don't kick dat blessed dead creature. Kick me, instead!"

The policeman looked as if he were willing to oblige but the gardener jumped between police foot and bawling maid, with the pretence of trying to calm her down.

"God bless Mr. Baps!" he babbled, his hand roaming over the curve of maid batty that quivered with every bogus sob. "Him was too good for dis world! Him must have give 'way all him money last night just before him dead! Him used to do dat all de time! Remember last year Easter, Mabel, when him give 'way a thousand dollar to dat beggar boy without foot at Half-Way-Tree?"

"Yes," Mabel shrieked. "Me remember! Me remember!"

"Who de rass dem talking 'bout, eh? I never give a 'beggar boy a penny in me life!"

"Me know dat, sah," Hopeton answered gloomily.

"Not to say dat I wasn't going to reform someday!" I hastened to add.

While the maid spilled eyewater and the gardener told lie after lie about my generosity, the policemen looked confused and unsure of themselves.

Finally one of the policemen ordered Mabel to cease and desist with the bawling and cover the dead body with a sheet while the other grumbled that now he'd seen everything—a Jamaican dropping dead with only a twenty dollar in his wallet—that this was what happened when you kept changing governments, for he remembered when Labour was in power that even the lowliest beggar on the street who dropped dead had at least a fifty dollar on his person.

Muttering to himself about how the IMF agreement had ruined the Jamaican economy, he went outside, saying he would radio for an ambulance to pick up the dead body.

"Mr. Baps was a saint!" Mabel pealed anew. "A saint!"

"Dey walk amongst us unacknowledged," the gardener brayed. "Some man just have a heart of gold, and nobody can see it 'til dem dead."

"Damn liars!" I bawled.

"I still say somebody thief government evidence," the remaining policeman glowered.

"Come Mr. Baps," Hopeton said, nudging me gently by the elbow. "Dis is earthly business. We on our way to heaven."

"How we going get dere?" I asked eagerly, hurrying after him onto the veranda and out into the front yard. "A chariot of fire?"

"No, sah," he replied. "A minibus."

Chapter 4

Me and this duppy boy had one beast of a row all the way to the bus stop.

I ranted and raved that it was out of order to expect a decent Jamaican to take a minibus to heaven, that if fiery chariot were not available, the least the appropriate authorities could do was to provide a late-model taxi. With minibus indiscipline running rampant on the Jamaican roadways, it was too much to expect a law-abiding citizen, a former teacher who had always driven his own private vehicle, to ride unruly public transportation to heaven. I raged that there was many a parson who, if they knew that the official transport to heaven was a minibus, would outright refuse to dead. For this a man spent a lifetime of Sundays wearing out his kneebone in church? He might as well go carouse and whore up himself in a rum bar.

Hopeton remarked that none of this applied to me since I had never set foot in church.

"Nevertheless," I grumbled, "you obviously don't know me or my strong points. For example, you probably don't know that I am a man who always observe de golden rule. And I could tell you dat if I'd known I'd end up riding to heaven in a minibus, I'd have flouted its backside."

He said that there was no record of me ever observing any rule.

"Dat just goes to show how much you know!" I shot back. "De golden rule I observe is 'never thief from a man unless he first thief from you.' And everybody who ever did business with me knew dat when it came to dis one rule, I was quite the stickler."

As this telling point struck home we trudged along in silence, for it was obvious that I had stumped the wretch. We continued quite a ways down the road before his brain could cook up even a lame reply. Finally he muttered that if we didn't ride a minibus, we'd have a long walk to the culvert.

I drew brake in the middle of the road just as a diesel truck roared through my bellybutton and careened recklessly down the street, nearly fricasseeing a corporeal peel-neck chicken. "Culvert? What culvert?"

He looked pained. "To get to heaven from Jamaica, Mr. Baps, we have to crawl through a culvert."

"I not crawling through no damn culvert at my age!" I roared. "I was not a bad Jamaican. I paid taxes. I denounced political tribalism and bogus voting. In forty-seven years of life I grind only five maid who work for me, and I fire only one for saying 'no'. Some Kingston barrister grind five maid a week and fire ten a month over 'no'. What I do dat I must ride minibus and crawl like mongoose through a culvert to get to heaven?"

"Mr. Baps," he announced wearily, "everybody in Jamaica get to heaven through de same culvert. From prime minister to electrician down to rude parson. It is de only way!"

"But what about de bright light and de dark tunnel and de sweet music?"

He mumbled that he didn't know what I was talking about.

So I told him about a television show I'd once seen featuring people who had died and been revived and how every one of them had testified that they felt themselves sailing through a dark tunnel and soaring towards a soothing white light while sweet music played in the background. Not a one of them had said a word about minibus and culvert.

He heaved a weary sight and explained that the people I had seen in the television show were Americans, and that the US government had indeed installed an automated portal for use by its deceased citizens. As independent Jamaicans, we had our own gateway to heaven. And it happened to be a special secret culvert.

"You know something," I barked gruffly, "I not going anywhere with you!"

I stormed across the noisy road and headed back towards my own house. He came racing after me, bawling at me to wait, saying that I didn't understand.

"Why should I go up dere when I can stay down here?" I snapped over my shoulder, walking through traffic, trees, hedges, fence, and a barking dog as my duppy body glided through all earthly obstruction and obstacle. He jumped in front of me and asked me what, above all things in the world, I liked doing best of all. I asked him if this was a riddle or a trick and he swore that it was a serious question.

I stopped in the middle of a neighbourhood backyard with the dog snarling and barking up a storm and considered my mind.

The truth was that best of all I liked keeping shop for the reason that it gave me the opportunity to impose discipline and fiscal restraint over ole negar. I could cut off the credit of ole negar when they spent too much or dun their backside when they paid too little. I could enforce good posture on my district by banning all leaning and slouching of ole negar youth against my doorway or counter, and every now and again—and this was the sweetest of all—I'd catch a clerk thiefing and get to fire her backside after raising a satisfying stink.

But as I stood there in the strange backyard with a dog trying its best to bite my duppy foot, I felt ashamed to admit that such down-to-earth pursuits were what I loved best. Even when I was alive, if someone had asked me what was my first love in life, I probably wouldn't have blurted out, "Ruling ole negar." And now that I was dead and a duppy, I felt that I should aspire to something more highbrow like listening to a Mantovani record or reading a fat book—I don't know why, I just felt queasy about admitting to a duppy angel that nothing in life sweeted me more than taking the rod of correction to rambunctious ole negar.

However, he must have used his angel brain on me for he grinned and said, "If ruling ole negar is you pleasure, Mr. Baps, we have plenty dat need ruling in heaven, too."

My ears pricked up instantly.

"Oh, yes?"

"Plenty, sah. All lacking in discipline and fiscal restraint."

"Plenty who want to trust sugar and saltfish even if dey failed to pay on account last week?"

"Thousands, sah. Hundreds of thousands."

"So you have shop in heaven, too, eh?"

"Plenty shop, sah. City shop, country shop, supermarket shop, bazaar, emporium, and cold supper shop."

"But dese country shops, dey not like earthly shops you find in Jamaica?"

"Oh, yes, sah. Down to cockroach and rat."

"Duppy fly, too?"

"Yes, sah. Plenty, plenty duppy fly."

Meantime, as we were chatting, the dog was biting at my duppy foot over and over again, and each time his teeth snapped harmlessly through my duppy shinbone, he snarled and got madder.

I looked down at him and asked Hopeton if biting dog abided in heaven, too, and he assured me that some Jamaicans could not relax without the tonic of an occasional dog bite, and if a biting dog was what I wanted to keep me happy, one would be provided. That was how heaven was: what you wanted you got. What you didn't want, you didn't get.

"So come with me, eh, Mr. Baps?" he pleaded. "I promise you, you goin' love heaven. And if you don't love it, you can migrate. And if you still don't love it after migration, you can always crawl back through de culvert and live on earth in de bush as a Jamaican duppy."

I thought about it while the dog kept gnawing savagely at my foot all the time keeping up with its rowdy barking.

"Now, for instance," I asked Hopeton, "if dis was a dog in heaven, could I give him a kick?"

"Oh, certainly, Mr. Baps," he assured me. "In fact, I going give you a little bonus. Kick dis one before we set off for heaven."

I don't know how Hopeton did it, but suddenly my right foot felt as solid as a yam post, and I gave the dog a good kick that sent the brute tumbling across the yard and made him yelp bloody murder.

The mistress of the house and the maid came rushing out of the kitchen to see what was wrong with their mongrel, who was cowering in the corner whining, and while the two of them speculated aloud about what could cause the beast to behave so, Hopeton and I sauntered through a backyard hedge and headed across the road for the bus stop.

"Is duppy kick him, Mum!" the maid was wailing behind us.

"Don't be an ass, Millicent! There's no such thing as duppy. And if there were, they don't kick."

"Duppy kick, Mum! And duppy love to kick dog!"

Sometime around midmorning we boarded a minibus crammed to the brim with passengers: knee and elbow jostled side by side for breathing room; nosehole found itself wedged in dangerous proximity to obnoxious battyhole and unaromatic crotch; arm, head and limb jutted out the windows and waved like surrender flag; ironed frock and fresh pants crease melted and wrinkled in the stuffy heat from the crush of bodies, while stale exhale and armpit exhaust made the stuffy interior stink like bat manure in a cave.

During the trip we suffered through the expected vehicular indiscipline, with the driver tailgating, weaving recklessly, screeching around corners, and driving like he owned the road.

I kept thinking to myself, "Now imagine, here I am dead and on my way to heaven in a minibus while this man drives recklessly with total disregard for the safety of the motoring public. Next thing you know he's going to cross Flat Bridge at an unsafe rate of speed and plunge into the river and drown everybody aboard, adding to de ole negar duppy population!"

Because he could see that I disapproved of this reckless driving, Hopeton leaned over from the cramped backseat where he was perched on the lap of a pretty brown woman who smelled of khus-khus perfume and asked if I would like him to administer a dose of duppy discipline to the driver.

I said that would make me very happy.

He reached over the seat and plunged his unwashed duppy hand straight into the driver's pot belly, twisting and turning with grunts of concentration while he tried to get a good grip on the man's gut. "Rass man eat too much pork rind," he griped. "Make him gut slippery."

Finally after much manoeuvring and squirming, Hopeton managed to pinch the colon, causing the driver to hiss a sudden, "Hi!" through his teeth.

Another tweak of duppy fingers and the driver winced and bellowed, "Whoa! I catch a stitch in my belly!"

Distracted by the stabbing pain in his colon, he slowed down to the speed limit and observed all traffic signs and appropriate cautions for the remainder of the trip. Hopeton withdrew his hand out of the man's belly and sucked air happily between his duppy teeth.

I thanked him for applying the needful discipline to an unruly driver and we drove on in silence, the roar of the engine blasting in our ears while I thought ruefully about all the money I had wasted during my lifetime on Milk of Magnesia and Epsom Salts.

Yet I could well imagine how people would laugh in my face if I came back and wrote that Jamaican bellyache was caused by duppy gripping you colon, and that the best thing you could do for it was to eat plenty pork rind to make your colon slippery to duppy grip.

They'd laugh so hard they'd pop.

Chapter 5

With our driver now practising motor vehicle courtesy and observing all road signs and applicable speed limits, our minibus ride on the Spanish Town Highway was cramped but uneventful.

As we neared our destination, Hopeton leaned over the front seat and whispered instructions into the ear of the driver, causing him to brake to a halt at the roadside shoulder next to the old Ferry Inn.

Hopeton signalled me to follow him out, which I did, climbing through the kneebones of bewildered passengers who looked around to see why the driver had stopped when none of them had asked to be let out and no one was waiting for a bus.

"Why you stop, driver?" croaked an old woman who was sandwiched miserably between two sweaty men in the back seat.

"I stop 'cause I feel to stop!" the man barked, turning around to glare at the multitudes crammed mutely behind him.

He stuck his head out the window, drew a cantankerous breath of canepiece breeze, smacked his lips and bawled to the world at large, "Now I driving off 'cause I feel to drive off!"

With that he revved the engine and roared away, but only after giving the appropriate signal with his indicator and looking both ways to ensure that it was safe to merge into the flow of traffic.

Hopeton slid down the embankment and strode off purposefully towards a canefield, warning me over his shoulder to please follow him closely.

It was a hot and dusty midmorning. We pushed into the thick cane growth and glided harmlessly through the sharp leaves. In the distance the Blue Mountain range was crumpled and pleated in purple shadows against the skyline. Overhead a John Crow unwound on a breeze. I am a man who has always appreciated nature and valued local beautification programmes, and even on my way to heaven, I took note of my surroundings. Butu, on the other hand, don't know bauble from bangle and bead.

We plodded past a cane cutter who was panting and sweating in the hot sun as he thinned out the stalks with a machete. Instinctively I said, "Good morning, sah!" which drew an amused chuckle from Hopeton along with a reminder that I was dead.

After walking a good distance we came to a rutted marl road and were about to cross when out of the canepiece oozed a fatty woman dressed in black and trailed by a harassed looking guide with whom she had evidently been quarrelling. Hopeton yelled to the man who answered eagerly and trotted over, both of them looking as pleased as higglers meeting up in the Miami airport.

"You catch one!" Hopeton exclaimed, shaking the man's hand.

"Catch one!" the woman bellowed roughly. "Please do not talk about me as if I'm a fish! Have some respect. I only just dead!"

"She miserable no rass," the man sighed to Hopeton out of his mouth corner. "And she say she not crawling through no damn culvert. I always get de troublesome ones."

"Troublesome ones?" Hopeton whispered. "You don't know troublesome yet. I had one man from St. Mary last week who tried to shoot me!"

"Go 'way! You too lie!"

With the two duppy guides talking shop and swapping stories at the fringe of the canepiece, I edged over to the woman and bade her a "good morning."

"I just dead," she said crossly. "Nothing good 'bout dis morning!"

"Well, I just dead meself. But now we on we way to heaven, thanks be."

"Heaven! Through a culvert? What kind o' heaven is dat?"

I tried to ease her fears but she would not be satisfied. She raved about being chucked on a minibus like she was a crocus bag of yam.

"Did you travel on a minibus, too, or did you get to ride in a proper fiery chariot?" she asked suspiciously.

I assured her that I, too, had suffered the indignity of minibus transport although my duppy had been good enough, at my request, to impose discipline on its driver.

"You see dat!" she boomed indignantly to her guide. "His driver was disciplined! But I had to ride with an indisciplined driver! Why Jamaicans must practise favouritism even after dey're dead, eh?"

Her guide had no answer to this inquiry, but merely glanced nervously over at her.

I invited the woman to sit down on the embankment and tell me about herself.

She snorted that dirty Jamaican soil had not come in direct contact with her law-abiding batty for well over a quarter-century and she didn't intend to give it the chance now just because she happened to be dead.

However, after much fuming and fussing she grudgingly told me her story.

She said that she was a decent churchgoing woman from Portland with no criminal record whatsoever, a homeowner with a substantial bank account, if it was any of my business; that this morning she had gotten up intending to attend church service—being an Adventist—and had just put on her finest frock when pain lick her in her belly and she keeled over dead. Next thing she knew, she said, there was this impertinent boy telling her she must ride a minibus at her age and crawl through a culvert to reach heaven. She said grimly that she had almost made up her mind not to go anywhere with the wretch, but he sweetmouthed her and begged her to follow him, which was how she found herself traipsing through a canepiece in the broiling sun when she could have been haunting various and sundry wretches in her parish and wreaking duppy revenge.

Finished with her story, she harrumphed crossly and began fanning herself with a kerchief.

"Hopeton say duppy can't feel heat," I remarked, staring at her makeshift fan.

"Stop calling me duppy! Me name is Eugenia Jones. I have me green card to America, and God only know why I didn't use it when I had de chance! I'd be sailing down a lighted tunnel right now instead of stomping through a stinking canepiece."

"We must make de best of things. Negativity can't help our common cause."

"Me and you have no common cause, sah! Is only dead we happen to dead together."

I shrugged and settled down on the embankment.

"How much longer you going keep decent people waiting in de hot sun?" she bellowed at the chatting guides, whereupon they immediately scurried to our side and we resumed our trek through the canefield.

We walked for another twenty minutes or so until we came to the dried-up watercourse of a straggly gully, which the guides clambered down briskly, drawing a protesting squawk from Eugenia, who had to be coaxed down it like a sore-foot heifer.

We resumed our walk in the blazing sun, marching down the gully mouth with no crunch underfoot and leaving no footprints in our wake. The sun beat down on us but drew no sweat.

"It look like duppy never need deodorant," I remarked for the sake of conversation.

"I can certainly smell you!" the cantankerous woman declared.

I was going to answer her but I exhorted myself, "Baps, don't let ole negar spoil you journey to de Heavenly Kingdom!"

So I held my peace and trudged at the rear of the group, taking my mark on the heifer rump that swayed and rocked ahead of me and threatened, with every twist and bend, to plug up the narrow gully mouth.

Half an hour of grim, speechless walking and we came to the culvert.

Milling about this most abandoned and unlikely spot for a portal to heaven were recently dead souls and their spirit guides, and a scattershot queue with neither discipline nor geometry to recommend it unravelled all over the canepiece. Men and women and a few children slouched and slumped in this line, energetically chatting.

Children darted in and out of the cane, romping and playing hide and seek, and a few of the more venturesome ones who had just mastered the art of duppy flying, filled the skies overhead, provoking the queued up adults with swooping, squealing dives as they playfully tried to knock the hats off the heads of the ducking women.

27

"Mind you fall, children!" one old woman was periodically bellowing at the dive-bombing children, who shrieked with joy as they skimmed the canepiece and plunged recklessly near the ground, swishing past the bobbing heads of the adults, some of whom swatted at them as they would at mosquitoes.

"Why you don't try and fly, too?" a woman teased another ahead of her in the line. The other kissed her teeth with contempt and replied tartly that just because she was dead was no reason for a decent woman to behave like a common bush bird.

From the general hubbub around me I overheard nearly universal criticism of the culvert, with many among the women griping that crawling through a drainpipe was bound to dirty up their frocks and make them enter heaven looking like street urchins. One woman gloated smugly about how glad she was that she had been wearing only a pair of old dungarees when she had been run over by a gravel truck, that she would have been very put out if she had to crawl through a culvert in her good frock.

Another fervently declared that she was grateful to God for allowing a gunman to shoot her down outside the beauty salon after she'd just gotten a perm, for at least her hair looked its best for entering heaven.

"Why I did have to dead first thing in de morning?" another woman carped. "Why I couldn't dead after I'd washed my face and combed my hair?"

Behind her stood an elderly dignified gentleman who grinned at the antics of the swooping children while listening with amusement to the grumbling women.

When one woman demanded to know what he found so funny, the old man murmured that after years of being bedridden with rheumatism and finding himself now able to walk without pain, he didn't care if to get into heaven he had to jump down the mouth of a pit toilet.

Even though we were all stone dead, there was such festivity and jubilation in the air, such a splatter of laughter and squeals combined with the shrieks of the romping children, that the canepiece rang with the excitement and babble of a duppy jamboree.

The line sputtered slowly forward as one by one the dead entered the culvert with their guides and disappeared, and soon I had inched up to the moment when it would be my turn.

A swirl of peering bodies surrounded the entrance to the culvert as some duppies became fainthearted at the last second and refused to take the crawl. They were huddled aside with their guides, who earnestly inveigled with them.

Standing stubbornly apart from the crowd was a woman with a parasol, who was shaking her head adamantly at her imploring guide. She was not crawling into no culvert, she blared. For all she knew, these so-called guides were demons funnelling them into hell. She bawled that from where she stood she definitely smelled brimstone coming from the culvert, which pronouncement caused a gasp of alarm from those near the head of the line.

A woman turned to me and worriedly asked if I smelled brimstone.

I sniffed the air carefully and said that I did not. Eugenia, however, began squealing at the top of her lungs, "Yes, is true! Dis culvert definitely smell of brimstone!"

Emitting a mass squeal of fear, the coiling head of the line shrank from the mouth of the culvert as if whipped by a blast of breeze.

"Dere is no brimstone smell!" a guide yelled over the noise of the fearful crowd. "De lady is mistaken! Dere is no hell!"

"Me don't trust no negar duppy," another woman declared grumpily.

"Please, you holding up de line!" a third guide cried over the confusion.

"I not crawling into hell, sah!" the woman who said she smelled brimstone declared. "I staying right here in Jamaica."

With that she hoisted her parasol and set sail across the canepiece with her guide trundling after her, begging her to reconsider.

"People, hear me!" bellowed a guide, who seemed to be the headman. "If you walk 'way like dat woman, you going roam Jamaica like a good-for-nothing duppy who live inna cotton tree! Dere is no brimstone! Dis is de path to heaven!"

The elderly gentleman stepped forward.

"I don't do nothing for de Lord to burn me in brimstone," he announced confidently. "If dis pipe lead to heaven, I am ready to enter."

"Good for you, sah!" the headman guide burst into a frenzied clapping, which was feebly taken up by other guides at his glowering prompting. "Step dis way, sah! Nothing to fear!"

The gentleman got down on his knees behind his guide and positioned himself at the mouth of the culvert for the crawl into heaven.

He chuckled. "Look at me with rheumatism crawling on hands and knees into heaven! I shoulda dead long time ago instead o' listening to fool-fool doctor. Good-bye, sah. See you in paradise."

With that he scurried energetically into the culvert as spry and frisky as a young lizard.

As the gentleman's feet slipped into the shadowy maw and disappeared, the headman broke into another frenzied clapping and scanned the teeming crowd, which was still eddying about dubiously. "Who's next? Dere's no brimstone! Ten seconds and you in heaven."

"You want to go before me, sah, go!" the woman in line ahead of me stood aside and saucily invited.

My heart was pounding madly as I cautiously leaned over and took another lingering sniff at the culvert.

The old gentleman had had a full head of white hair and I reasoned that if this pipe led to hell, I should at least smell hair being singed. But I smelled nothing but the faint odour of cane drying in the sun.

Mumbling at Hopeton to please excuse me for a moment, I stepped from the head of the line and strolled away from the crowd into the canefield where I could have privacy. I had just ducked into the thick green stalks when I saw Hopeton's anxious face peering at me through the blades.

"Mr. Baps," he croaked nervously, "don't run 'way from me now, sah!"

"If you must know," I snapped, "I came to say good-bye to me hood."

"You hood going on a journey, sah?"

"Don't be a jackass! Everybody know dat hood don't abide in heaven."

"Oh, no, sah! In Jamaica heaven, hood thrive and prosper with no superannuation!"

I stared sharply at the wretch, wondering if he was lying to me.

"No shearing of hood take place at heavenly gate?"

"Who tell you dat lie, Mr. Baps?"

"A nun."

He said, "Oh," and proceeded to assure me that although the churches had been pushing for centuries in favour of compulsory shearing of hood at heaven's gate, the government had repeatedly said that no such policy would ever be implemented—and as a Jamaican, I should know that no government minister would ever vote to part with his beloved hood.

"So what you say now, Mr. Baps?" he asked eagerly.

I swallowed hard. "I say, let's go to heaven!"

"Yes, sah!" he practically bawled out in my ears, and we trotted briskly to the head of the line where the crowd was still darting and swirling around the mouth of the culvert.

"Make way," Hopeton barked officiously, elbowing his way through the people who were circling the culvert mouth and warily sniffing it for brimstone, "Mr. Baps bound for heaven."

Squinting to accustom my eyes to the light, I got down on hands and knees and followed Hopeton who was crawling ahead of me. As soon as I was completely inside the dim and narrow pipe, I felt a strong draft sucking me into the walls.

"It breezy in here!" I cried to Hopeton, and just as the words were out of my mouth, I was swirled against the rough concrete pipe and sucked through its walls as if by a strong undertow. Before I could even blurt out, "Back foot!" I felt my body seep through the concrete pipe and ooze out onto the other side where it settled on a grassy hillside in a puddle of duppy flesh.

I was clambering shakily to my feet, trying to get my bearings, when I heard a diabolical shriek right in my ears, "You stinking brute, you! You finally reach!" and a woman looming nearby flung a huge rockstone straight at my head and knocked me murderously off my feet.

"Lawd Jesus!" I gasped as I fell backwards. "Mad woman murder me in heaven! Me dead again! "

Chapter 6

Like many Jamaican boys of my generation, I was brought up to believe that in order to become a decent man it was necessary for various adults to lick me down several times a year. Now that I am grown, I look back fondly on this child rearing philosophy, which I did not fully value as a stupid youth who was being regularly licked down. But you grow up, learn proper values and take on a new perspective on life.

Once, after I was already in my forties, I remember meeting up with one of my old teachers at a dance and going over to congratulate him on busting a slate over my ten-year-old head during a difficult arithmetic lesson. I explained to him that after I had recovered from concussion, I not only knew all my multiplication tables, I had mastered long division as well, which I credited to his tutorial braining. Scowling, he took what I said the wrong way and warned that if I didn't stop persecuting him he would summon a constable. And no matter how hard I tried to assure him that I was not being sarcastic or cynical, he refused to take credit for his arithmetic clubbing.

But even with this vast experience, never had I ever tasted a lick as sweet as when that strange woman busted my head beside the culvert of heaven. It sweeted me so that I could only flutter on the grass and shiver in spasms of sheer deliciousness.

As I lay there quivering, souls continued to seep through the culvert and liquefy on the grass in duppy flesh that curdled, stood upright, and marvelled in outbursts of jubilation and excitement. I heard gasps and ejaculations erupting around me—salvos of "Watch dis now!" "Rass! Look 'pon de clouds!" or "Kiss me neck!

How de grass so green?" or "Marva! Is you dat?" or "What a way you hard to dead, eh, Lincoln?" and various babbling of this kind from the milling throng of newcomer duppies.

Barely conscious, I was awash in laughter, giggling, cries, whistles, and exclamations of astonishment and joy. Women squealed, reunited family members chattered, longdead husbands and newly dead wives hugged and kissed joyfully, and old mothers greeted their arriving grown children with noisy merrymaking. And all this public commotion broke over me in waves of sound as I wallowed ecstatically on the grass, shivering from the sweetness of a busted head.

Hopeton shoved between me and my attacker, who gaped down at me with bewilderment.

"Miss Daisy!" he bawled. "You lick down de wrong man again!"

"Sorry, sah!" she apologised to me, helping me regain my feet. "Me did think you was me husband."

Reeling and groggy, I asked her if I was dreaming or if she'd really licked me down with a rockstone.

She looked embarrassed and said that she had indeed licked me down. She explained that she had mistaken me for her dirty, lowdown husband who, no sooner had she been buried last year, began carousing with nasty women all over St. Mary, and when the mangy dog got to heaven she was going to teach him to grind other women in her matrimonial bed while she rotted in her grave like a respectable wife.

Hopeton grumbled at Miss Daisy about her habit of licking down strange men at the culvert of heaven, saying that it wasn't her first offence and he was getting sick and tired of her assault on decently deceased people, and what kind of impression was she making for heaven

35

when the first thing a newly arrived soul felt was her rockstone cracking open his skull. The woman growled that she had already said she was sorry and body could do no better. Then she scuttled back to her post at the mouth of the culvert where she could scan the souls who were periodically oozing out of it and puddling onto the grounds of heaven, her rockstone held menacingly aloft as she prepared to ambush the gallivanting husband.

"Mr. Baps!" Hopeton called at me to follow him.

I told him that I was coming and paused to take my first look at the land called heaven.

I beheld before my eyes a land whose every leaf, twig and grass blade glittered with a spanking shininess as if all the shimmering earth had just been carefully buffed. Throughout the grassy hillside were trees and shrubs and bushes that sparkled like Christmas ornaments, and all the land looked as new as a just unwrapped toy.

"Come, Mr. Baps!" Hopeton urged again, for I was standing dumbstruck by the scenic loveliness and savouring the coolness of the mountain breeze that swirled and fanned against my cheeks. Reluctantly I ambled after Hopeton along with other recently arrived souls who also gambolled down the rolling hillside chattering to their guides as excitedly as children at a birthday party.

"What a way dat rockstone lick sweet, Hopeton!" I marvelled, scampering to his side as we headed briskly towards the distant green valley.

Hopeton grunted. "Wait till a madman chop off you head with a machete! Now if you want something sweet, dat is really sweet."

"You mean you have rampaging madman in heaven, too?"

He chuckled. "Mr. Baps, everything you have on earth we have up here, too. Only better."

We were halfway down the slope leading to the valley when behind us we heard a hollow blow explode and a guide's voice indignantly bellowing, "Woman! You lick down a Jehovah Witness!" followed by the now familiar apologetic mumble, "Sorry, sah. Me did think you was me stinking husband!"

We trekked through the bushland of heaven. Prickle raked at our bodies but drew no blood. The sun gleamed overhead, the land smelled robust and earthy, and my heart brimmed with an indescribable gladness. I kept scolding myself for having wasted forty-seven years of life on frowzy earth when all along I could have been revelling in heaven. I kept repeating to myself, "Baps, you not really dead, dis is a dream!"

But then I would immediately answer myself, "Woe, Baps! You well dead! Dis is no dream!"

I tried to make conversation with Hopeton as we glided through the bushland but he was intent on getting me to the registry station so he could return to Jamaica to fetch another soul. He mumbled hurriedly that he had at least two other souls due for pickup today, and that one of them was a politician from whom he anticipated difficulty.

As we followed the winding country path I noticed that I was acquiring solidity, that my belly was returning to its usual robustness, and that my complexion was once again regaining its rich dark fleshiness. I asked Hopeton what was happening and he said that I was experiencing heavenly clumping and regaining my solid form.

I lifted up my shirt to examine my body for signs of clumping. My belly was smooth and solid and a bushy patch of hair again sprouted in a thick row from my groin to my chest. But there was one thing peculiar that I immediately felt as I ran my hands over my front: I had no belly-button.

"Where me belly-button?" I asked Hopeton, who was leading us through a leafy grove.

"You don't need dat in heaven," he said over his shoulder.

I said "Oh," and put my hands into my pockets to see whether my hood was still made of duppy gas and even as I groped I could feel with a thrill that my balls had once more been wholesomely clumped.

"Merciful heavens be thanked!" I muttered.

My indoor parson bawled, "Baps, you dog! Don't gloat over clumping of hood! Hood don't business in heaven!"

We walked on through the dreamy loveliness of the countryside, my heart so strong and exultant that I bounded over rocks and roots like a frisky goat who had just gobbled down a wayside ganja bush. And as we walked I kept rejoicing that I was skipping through the bushland of heaven, while all around me sparkled the wondrous splendour of paradise.

Yet something bothered me, and as we walked down the shady woodland path I asked Hopeton, "Where de sheep?"

"What sheep?" he flung gruffly over his shoulder.

"How you mean 'what sheep'? De sheep dat safely graze, of course!"

He said if I wanted sheep, I would get sheep, and I tried to explain to this former housebreaker that it wasn't a question of what I wanted or didn't want, but heaven without sheep was clearly out of order. "You need sheep, man, if you want a true heaven!"

No sooner had I spoken than I heard a tremulous, melodic baaing wafting from the underbrush.

"Listen!" I cried excitedly.

Hopeton pushed through the undergrowth into a spacious clearing and on the fringes of the encircling woodlands I spotted a fluffy, white sheep baaing sweeter than any barble dove. It wasn't the nasal noise of earthly sheep that baaed with an American twang and made a man want to stew every one of them down into mutton broth, but a kind of birdlike cooing that made me feel to dance.

I was beginning to shake to the rhythm when a rockstone flew from behind a bush and clouted the warbling sheep on the head, licking it down onto the grass.

"Who lick down me sheep?" I bawled, rushing over to find a white man dressed in a business suit skulking behind a bush. But before he could answer the sheep jumped to its feet baaing as sweetly as the Mormon Tabernacle Choir.

Hopeton broke into a broad grin at the sight of the white man.

"Mr. Philosopher," Hopeton teased, "you lick a sheep down. You concede you alive and in heaven now?"

The white man sniffed and mumbled that he hadn't meant to lick him down, for he knew the sheep didn't exist, and that he didn't exist, that nobody in this particular clearing existed—neither did the clearing for that matter, nor the shrubs, trees, bushes, grass and flowers—but his ears found no sound more gruesome than the baaing of sheep, even one that didn't exist. When he heard the phantom baa he couldn't control himself, he just felt to kill the ugly baaing bitch rather than put up with its noise in his ears which, by the way, didn't exist either.

All this the philosopher rambled in a listless monotone as he twiddled a twig between his fingers.

I was stunned. "You saying I, Taddeus Baps who just dead and reach heaven, don't exist?"

"Who is Taddeus Baps?" he wondered, peering up sluggishly at me.

"Me! Myself! I! Alive and up in heaven!"

"There is no Baps," he said dispiritedly, cracking a twig between his fingers like the wishbone of a chicken.

"Dere is Baps!" I shrieked, feeling to kick the brute.

"Come, Mr. Baps," Hopeton tugged at my sleeve. "We just need to climb dat hill and we reach. De politician get shot already and a doctor about to finish him off. I have to run."

"There is no hill," the white man mumbled. "There is no politician."

We moved away, leaving him behind his bush. I asked Hopeton what a white foreigner was doing up here all by himself. Hopeton muttered that I shouldn't get too vexed at the poor soul, for he used to be a famous American philosopher who had written books saying that upon death everyone evaporated into molecules and now that he was dead he stubbornly refused to admit that he was wrong and in heaven and all he did was roam through the bush awaiting his moment of evaporation.

As we climbed a sloping pasture and trudged towards a country shop sitting against a hillside, I sputtered angrily, unable to get over the nerve of the wretch, "De brute deserve evaporation! I can understand saying dere is no heaven! But to say dere is no Baps!"

Chapter 7

It was a perfect country shop—in the sense a woman means when she calls a man a "perfect brute."

Perched like a grass tit's nest on the edge of the road, it boasted just the right mix of ramshackle, grime, and stink, and might have been glimpsed anywhere sagging pitchy-patchy against a hillside on earthly Jamaica.

We stepped onto the shaky wooden floor of the porch past a mauger dog who bared a dose of teeth at us as we skirted him and entered the smelly interior.

Inside, slouched behind the counter and squinting at a newspaper, was a big, fatty woman whose frizzy head was bound with a calico wrap and speckled by a swarm of flies. She glanced up at our footsteps and beamed at Hopeton.

"You catch anodder one!" she roared boisterously, creasing the paper and laying it to one side as she prepared to transact official business.

"How you do, Miss B?" Hopeton greeted her courteously, adding with a nod that, yes, he was bringing in a newly dead Jamaican duppy for heavenly registration, but he was in a hurry and could she please look up the name "Taddeus Baps" in the official government book of arriving souls and sign a receipt crediting my delivery to his account.

Miss B plodded into the dingy back room and returned lugging a bulky ledger which she opened on the counter and began scanning.

After scouring several pages, she stung me with a doubtful glance and muttered, "I have a 'Daps,' but no 'Baps'. Dis man not dead."

"Kiss my backside!" I exploded indignantly. "I most certainly am dead! Nobody in dis shop is deader dan me!"

"You bring dis undead man to carry on bad in me peaceful shop, Hopeton?"

"I must carry on bad for I know dat I am well dead! So dead dat even me maid and garden boy pick bonus money outta me pocket dis very morning! And anytime employee bonus money flow outta my pocket into ole negar hand, it can only mean one thing: dat I am most definitely dead!"

A rind of silence intruded between us in the shop as we glared at each other. Hopeton scraped the creaky wooden floor with his shoe and mumbled, "Is true, Miss B. Dis is a man who would really dead before him pay bonus."

I had a sudden suspicion. "What is de first name of de man 'Daps'?"

Miss B sullenly turned the pages of the book and ran her finger down the stack of names. "Taddeus Daps."

"Of what address?"

She rattled off my address.

"Dat's me! Dey misspell me name. Nobody live at dat address but me, Taddeus Baps. And nobody dead dere today but me."

She strained to read the floral script in which the name was written, turned the book and shoved it towards me on the counter for me to read that the "B" of my name was written to resemble a "D," growling that a Rural Registration Officer certainly could not be held accountable for illegible government penmanship.

Seeing the misunderstanding on the verge of being cleared up, Hopeton hastily shook my hand and scampered out of the shop, saying that he had to run for the dead politician had begun haunting Gordon House and the Leader of the Opposition was preparing a speech denouncing parliamentary duppy as the newest government dupe.

With that he scurried out the door, across the street, and into the hillside thicket.

I ran onto the porch and bawled after him, "But what am I supposed to do now?" to which he flung back over his shoulder, "Miss B will fix you up!" just before he skidded out of sight into the thick bush.

From inside the shop Miss B barked, "Come Mr. Baps! Or Mr. Daps! Or whatever you name! You have plenty paper to sign."

I had to sign that I had arrived in heaven safely, that no injury had befallen me along the way, that my guide had been courteous and cooperative, that my passing had been altogether to my liking and that if it wasn't, I would indemnify the Jamaican government from any liability in connection thereof and would file no lawsuit.

"Now, say dat dey hang me at Spanish Town gallows," I put a case to Miss B, who had propped her unkempt belly roll against the counter as she pushed form after form under my nose, "how could I sign a paper saying I like dat passing?"

"Dey sign, though," she rumbled like an old bus. "No matter if dey dead from ptomaine, rockstone, gunshot or hanging."

"Anybody ever refuse to sign?"

She nodded and said, yes, there had been one man, a government surveyor from St. Mary, who had died while catching a grind from a young primary schoolteacher in the bush, and who had steadfastly refused to sign the paper, grumbling that to dead while riding a woman at the base of a breadfruit tree was not his idea of a satisfactory passing and he intended to hold higher-ups responsible for such shoddiness.

Finally, the signing was done, or at least I thought it was, for Miss B began putting away the papers in a manila envelope.

"One final question," she asked gruffly, fumbling with a dog-eared form. "You want to keep you hood?"

I was shocked by this ill-mannered question, but for the sake of argument I asked her to explain.

She rolled her eyes and sighed and said that if I were a staunch Christian and desired to live hoodless in heaven, I had to fill out this form, checking off the hoodless box, and then travel to Kingston after the ministry had notified me of an appointment with a licensed hood remover. On that said day my earthly hood would be painlessly removed leaving behind not even a scrap of pubic hair—everything shaved clean. I asked what if I were a woman, and she replied that in such a case my pumpum would be caulked by a licensed pumpum caulker.

With that, she sullenly flicked the form across the counter. I made no move to pick it up.

"Nobody troubling me hood," I mumbled.

She chuckled and looked pleased as she put away the form. "Boy, Jamaican man just love dem hood, eh? Even in heaven, dem don't change!"

And she winked lewdly at me from where she perched on the counter stool, floating on a tube of roly-poly batty flesh.

Where would I sleep? What would I do? Where would I work? How would I occupy my days?

Just this morning I had had clear answers to these common questions, but now that I was dead and in heaven, I had to wonder.

Miss B returned to her reading while I stood around in the shop feeling useless and out of place and wondering what was supposed to happen next.

I cleared my throat. "Now what?"

"You dead and reach heaven. Enjoy youself," she advised indifferently, her frizzy head ducked deep inside the open paper.

"How? Doing what?"

"Whatever you want!"

"Nothing happen today like it say in scripture. You don't even look like an angel. Angel not supposed to be so meaty."

"I am not a damn angel!" she growled, peering up crossly at me and sounding vexed. "I am a Jamaican! If you want angel, you have to migrate to America and join sheep heaven."

Since I was getting nowhere with her, I looked around at the dinginess of the smelly shop, the slapdash jumble of bakery items and canned goods that cluttered the rickety shelves, the dirty coil of wooden counter behind which she sat reading, and felt a sudden urge to bring order and discipline to the mess.

Strolling to the far end of the counter, I impulsively began restacking the goods and dusting the shelves, trying to do so as quietly as possible so as not to disturb Miss B. But it was impossible, for she was sitting right under my nose as I worked.

"You dead to come dust off de shelf of my shop and restack me goods without permission?" she growled, peering up from her newspaper.

"No. Dat is not de reason I specifically dead. But I owned three shops on earth before I dead. And I don't like idleness."

She stared at me long and hard. Finally she scowled and returned to her paper muttering under her breath, "Rass man just dead and reach heaven and him come take over me shop! Boy, negar duppy really have gall!"

But even as she grumbled she became engrossed in the paper, which I took as her permission to proceed.

I found a rag and began to scrub and wipe the shelves until I could see the grain of the wood. Then I stood on a crate and repacked the tinned goods neatly by type, restoring order to disarray and clutter.

Some customers occasionally wandered in while I worked, many of them exchanging idle talk and afternoon pleasantries with Miss B as they helped themselves by reaching over the counter and plucking canned goods off the shelf with no payment or accounting other than a cheerful, "Put it down in de book, Miss B!" before they sailed out of the shop, laden down with merchandise.

One woman tried to grab a tin of bully beef out of my hand as I was stacking it on the shelf, but I held on firmly and refused to give it up.

"Miss B," she cried out, playing tug-of-war with me, "will you tell dis damn man to leggo de tin o' bully beef!"

"Give her de bully beef," Miss B muttered, hardly glancing up from her paper.

"Not a backside!" I roared. "First de goods must stack. Den customers can purchase dem. Plus, I don't see no money in her hand!"

Miss B glowered at me before climbing down off her stool, stomping to the shelf I was stacking, extracting a tin of bully beef and handing it to the woman, who put it in her purse with the usual chirp, "Put it down in de book, Miss B!" as she disappeared out the door throwing me a dirty look.

"Woe, Baps!" my parson bawled. "Dis is rampant Manley socialism!"

After I had finished cleaning the shelves and restacking the goods, I stood aside and admired my handiwork.

Miss B, who had gone onto the veranda to gossip with a neighbour, waddled into the shop, peered at what I had done, and led me to a small back bedroom where she said I could spend the night, adding that she had not asked for my help and that she had been perfectly content with her shop before I interfered with it. I nodded politely and refused to be drawn into a senseless argument and, instead, stepped out onto the front porch of the shop, intending to take in the cool evening air.

The rickety veranda on which I stood was perched on the edge of a narrow country road that looped around a slab of mountainside before slithering down a steep curve. Ridging the distant twilight skies was a lumpy green mountain range dotted with cultivator plots and scattered shacks whose windows sparkled with yellow lights. Smoke uncoiled from a woody pleat somewhere deep within the mountain and was braided into lazy, twisting tresses of good hair by a soft breeze.

The evening was lovely as I strolled the one narrow street past rows of shops and small dwellings, bidding the occasional villager "Good evening."

Soon I was rambling in the gathering dusk down a country lane while groundswells of guinea grass crested and glistened in tree-lined fringes on either side of the narrow road. A recent sprinkle of rain had fallen and the scent of cleanliness and freshness wafting off the earth made me feel lighthearted.

When I returned to the shop, Miss B was gone and the premises deserted.

I retired into the back room, took off my clothes and lay down in the bed listening to the peaceful night sounds drizzling against the window.

The day had been long and trying. Dying had taken a lot out of me, and I felt quite drowsy.

No bed is sweeter than one in a Jamaican mountain village, and it took me no more than a yawn before I dropped off into a refreshing slumber.

And it seemed no more than a twitch before I awoke from a dream of being ridden by a rampaging hippopotamus. I was squirming and wriggling to squirt out from under hippopotamus oppression when I opened my eyes and found myself pinned under fatty Miss B naked atop me and rumbling wheezily like a leaky steamroller.

"What you think you doing?" I sputtered.

"Grinding you," she grunted in my right ear.

"I tell you I want a grind?"

"Want it or not, you getting a grind."

"Fatty woman don't turn me on!"

"Dis is heaven. Every woman turn on every man. All woman have to do is jump on and the table spread and ready."

"I not spread! I not ready!"

"You well spread. And you plenty ready."

As Miss B spoke, she was humping up a jamboree and her wriggling and jiggling was so powerful that soon found myself clinging to beefy batty for dear until the two of us exploded simultaneously on the bed with a noisy bellowing, after which she collapsed atop me with a juicy hiss that blew down my earhole and clean out my big toenail.

A moment of restful silence followed during which we moistened each other's neck string with damp breath in the darkness.

"Dis is de first good ride I ever get from a fatty," I praised her, panting for breath.

She sighed and shifted, causing a watery mound of cool, naked beef to slush atop my body.

"I going do it again!"

"You mad? I done for de night."

"In heaven man don't done until woman say so."

"All dis riding going make me feel like a donkey!" I managed to sputter as she renewed the jiggling.

She scoffed. "You don't see donkey yet. You soon see donkey."

Chapter 8

My first night in heaven Miss B gave me twenty-five super-duper grind before a frothy morning light curdled against the window of the small room. After time number twenty I heard myself gasping, more from shock than from real fatigue, "You right! I didn't see donkey yet! But I see donkey now!"

Miss B chuckled and started up on lap number twenty-one.

The spate of super-duper grinding went throughout much of the morning, and at one point with Miss B grunting like she was getting clubbed, a woman from the village entered the store and cried, "Miss B? You back dere? I want some flour."

Miss B bawled out brazenly in my earhole, "I grinding Baps, Cynthia. Serve youself."

After a delicate hesitation from the shop, the customer answered with a mirthful cackling, "When you done, I can grind Baps, too?"

"If anything left when I finish!"

"Dis is heaven, Miss B! You know it never use up here, even after all sisters share it! Hallelujah!"

"Glory be!" Miss B blathered her agreement into my ear, heaving tirelessly.

I grumbled that she was giving me a bad name in the village, that I was one man who didn't broadcast my conjugal habits to the general public, but Miss B advised me to hush up and enjoy pumpum in heaven, and even as she said this, she made me bawl out loud and lusty with sheer joy over her juiciness, which caused the sister in the shop to chortle her congratulations, "Yes, Sister B! Dat's a good one!"

"Number twenty-four! I going for me quarter century!"

"I taking de flour. Later, Miss B! Enjoy de grind, Baps!"

"Thank you!" I managed to blubber politely, and just then Miss B rubbed up vigorously against me and I discovered to my surprise that she had a belly-button.

"How come you have a belly-button and I don't?" I asked curiously, sinking my thumb into its squishiness.

"You grow it back up here. When you belly-button ripe and full, you ready to born again."

"Born again? Why born again?"

"After you in heaven for a set time, you must born again to control de population and give anodder man a chance. You return to earth to live and dead again, den you come back up for another stay. Dat's how heaven run."

"But how long you get to stay up here? And how you know when is you time to go back down? And where dem send you down there?"

"How me fe know all dat? All I know is what I hear. Dem say when you time come you go back inna whichever baby borning in whichever part of de world, is dere you go."

"Even if de climate cold? Like, a man like me who love warm breeze, me couldn't born again inna Iceland, or one o' dem cold place?"

"Hush up, man! You asking too much question."

"But me no want born again in no cold climate!"

"Dat not you worry right now, for I going for number twenty-five."

"Mercy!"

****

In the days that followed I learned a lot about the village of heaven in which I now resided contentedly as a newly arrived duppy.

The shop was perched on the slopes of a green mountain daily awash in freshening breezes. I dwelled in a land where the sun shone bright but did not burn, where the deep cool nights were bejewelled with starlight and the mountain air always tasted sweet.

Yet the village also had the usual customs, habits, and sights we know and love on earthbound Jamaica.

So village dog was properly mauger but not mangy; village donkey brayed crossly but did not kick down children at garden parties; village busha reigned over hilltop but could not work black man to death in the hot sun at a thiefing wage; and village sister backbit every reputation in the district but was not compulsorily ugly.

Heaven is also a land where you can look exactly the way you wish. You can transform into any shape, form, or colour you prefer, can crimp your eye like a Chiny, straighten your hair like an Indian, bleach your skin like a white man, or turn as scrawny as a mosquito.

One day the subject of Miss B's big belly came up, and I asked her bluntly why she continued to resemble a breeding Red Poll cow when she could just as easily look like better, but she growled that she happened to love herself black and fat, which was why she hadn't availed herself either of government bleaching or thinning. She boastfully declared that she liked being beefy, loved her jelly belly, and was perfectly content to perch on her stool and float on a tube of batty fat. She challenged me to say that a fatty wasn't a comfortable, smooth ride and better by far than any bony woman, and I mumbled that certainly, much positive could be said in favour of womanly beefiness. She glared at this wishy-washy answer and I muttered sheepishly that being no expert on female fattiness, I wasn't the right one to ask.

She flew into a tirade and demanded to know if she hadn't made me come fifty-five times last night? Could a bony woman have accomplished as much? I said with dignity that I didn't see how such a thing was possible.

"I practice fatty power!" she cockadoodledooed.

I had thought Miss B was brazen and rude in her ways but I soon found out that in heaven there is no shame, expulsion, or favouritism practised on the human body, no apartheid of bodily parts such as we have on earth where a woman will earnestly declare in public, "Cross me heart!" but will sooner dead than say, "Cross me pumpum!" But that is exactly what a decent woman might spontaneously avow in heaven, where pumpum and hood worship in church as respected members of the congregation.

One day Miss B announced that she wanted me to attend church with her on Sunday. I objected that since I was now in heaven, I was in no further need of churching, but she replied that reaching heaven had nothing to do with church—Jamaican people just loved to jump up in church on Sundays and would continue to do so even if they were in hell. She informed me that she liked going to church on Sundays; furthermore, next week I was going, too.

True to her word the next Sunday Miss B hauled me off to a village church.

The service commenced with a hymn, to which I contributed a dutiful croak. I was right in the middle of singing "By the River of Babylon" when, to my horror and astonishment, Miss B reached over and wantonly patted my crotch like a parson feeling up a collection bag to see if it was fat.

I hissed that she was being out of order in a house of worship and drew away. Miss B whispered that she had been moved by the spirit, adding that in heaven all body parts—from hood to eyebrow—participated fully and equally in formal worship.

We had a furious mouth-corner argument.

I indignantly maintained that my hood had had a good upbringing and had been raised to sneak out at night only in canepieces, behind a bush, in unlighted bedrooms, or in the back seat of a car hunched in the shadows of a country road; that it never came out on a public street unless drawn out by an unruly streetwalker in the middle of a heated dispute over price. Miss B coolly advised me to look around, and when I did I beheld that a sister racked by the spirit would joyously reach over and knead the privates of any convenient elder. I also saw that the elders patiently endured this ecstatic groping without raising objection or lodging complaint, many even smiling indulgently at these sisterly antics.

But I was determined that no woman would seize hold of my hood while I was in church without observing appropriate restriction. I whispered to Miss B, as she sidled up to me once again, that since it was evidently the custom and I was a stranger to the district and did not wish to depart from tradition, I would permit an inspirational feel-up during the service when the spirit moved her, but not while she clutched the hymnal. She hissed that this was a ridiculous colonial regulation, adding that she didn't intend to draw out my hood into open air to play patty cake with it, she only wished to express her joyfulness by giving it a worshipful squeeze.

But I was firm: it was either hood or hymnal, not both. With a sigh, Miss B was therefore forced to reluctantly put down the hymn book whenever she felt moved by the spirit to paw me up, even though she fiercely rebuked me afterwards for fostering a backward colonial mentality.

For a good while—I don't know how long, for time is hard to keep track of in heaven—Miss B and I lived in contentment. I helped her around the house and shop during the days. Come evening time, she would cook for me, boiling up some serious dumpling and giving me fatty pumpum like it was locusts during the days of the Egyptian plague. During these happy times, no man in heaven was happier or slept sweeter than I, Taddeus Baps.

Sometimes at the end of the day, as Miss B was locking up, she would turn and bawl over her shoulder, "Baps, do me a favour! Run 'round to Miss Simpson and give her a good grind. When you reach back, honey-bunch, you supper will be ready. I cooking up some fry fish and bammy for you."

In this way, she would occasionally lend me to Miss Johnson or Miss Shirley or Miss Higgins, who were her sturdy church sisters and quite used to sharing among themselves such staples as sugar, flour, hood, and tinned milk, making me occasionally feel like the district grinding post. Of course, I could have refused, for there is no slavery in heaven, but that would have made me into nothing better than a worthless dog-in-the-manger.

So I did as I was told, and everyone was happy. Only my indoor parson was cross at this state of affairs, and one night as I was walking home from Miss Higgins' house down a dark and bushy country lane, I heard him fuming, "Dis heaven is a land of pumpum and dumpling. I wonder if we in hell?"

So things were running nicely between me and Miss B and everything was prospering.

Then one night I got the shock of my life, and everything between us suddenly mash up.

I had been peacefully snoozing on Miss B's belly in the dingy back room, the croaking lizards, crickets, and whistling frogs lullabying me into the blissful sleep of the fully satisfied fornicator. I had enjoyed a long and sweet belly ride and had spent the past three hours toasting in the cosy creaminess of her blubber. She had been drowsily urging me to confess that when it came to lovemaking and reign over the connubial bed a fatty was total queen, and I was in the middle of a good-humoured joshing with her about it when suddenly I had the funny feeling that the tip of her head was being noiselessly sawed off.

It was puzzling to see a woman's head disappearing in neat sections and I stared long and hard at her until her brow was almost all gone before I gave a gasp of alarm and remarked casually that in the bad light it looked as if her headtop was disappearing.

Miss B catapulted upright. She flung me savagely off her belly and onto the floor, and groped wildly at her head. "Rass!" she bawled. "I crowning!"

"Crowning?" I sputtered from the floor, where she had pitched me.

"I getting born again, Baps!" she shrieked.

As she bellowed her anguish, she began frantically plucking at her head which, before my eyes and in the glow of the night sky, was being cleanly sheared off like a cucumber chopped by an unseen cleaver.

"Help me!" she yelled.

"How? Wha' happening?"

"I sliding through a birth canal. Grab me foot and pull me back."

Jumping off the floor, I seized hold of her fleshy calves and began a fierce tugging that did nothing to slow the ghastly sectioning.

"I can't stop you!" I cried helplessly, as her entire head vanished, leaving only a fatty neck stump wobbling headless atop her tree-trunk chest.

"I don't want to born again!" Miss B howled, her voice echoing as if she were wedged in a narrow tunnel.

She had slid down past her bosom by now and even as I strained to hold onto her kicking legs her thighs oozed out of sight with a nasty gurgling, leaving me grappling with two slippery and twitching feet. With a vicious kick they were suctioned violently from my grasp and her whole body had disappeared.

"Miss B?" I cried aloud to the empty room.

I heard nothing but the high-pitched piping of insects outside the window. When I turned up the flickering kerosene lantern not even a coil of pubic hair remained of Miss B.

I sat down heavily on the bed, wondering what to do next, when suddenly in the jitterbugging lantern glow Miss B's face broke the surface of the pillowcase and wavered there as if afloat in the puddle of linen.

"Is all right, Baps!" the face whispered. "I going back as a Jamaican! I borning again in St. Elizabeth! Hallelujah!"

"Request a change of venue to St. Ann! St. Elizabeth is a fart of a parish!"

"Hush you mouth, Baps!" she scolded patriotically.

"Miss B! I goin' talk to God! I goin' beg him to ease you up!"

She chuckled as if at a private joke. "God don't have nothin' to do wid dis, Baps. Walk good, me love!"

With the final burbling gasp of a drowning swimmer, she squinched up her face, closed her eyes, and rippled below the pillowcase.

"Miss B?" I cried, rubbing the spot where her face had just been afloat.

Blown on the wind as if from a distance, I heard a sharp slap followed by the shrill wail of a newborn infant and the sleepy grumbling of a midwife, "De pickney don't want to born into dis wicked world!"

Chapter 9

"Well, Baps, it look like you catch a heavenly shop!"

After a refreshing night's sleep, that was the encouraging thought that popped into my head first thing the next morning.

For to tell the truth, in spite of Miss B's violent rebirth, I had slept as soundly as an evangelist who had spent the night wrestling a big-boned church organist against a bedpost. This was not heartlessness, but the nature of heaven where no heart can feel troubled or heavy or lost, and every soul can do exactly what it wants because every wish or whim is cheerfully granted. Only the time or place of rebirth is not under a soul's control.

I will give you a case in point.

In the village there was a youth who, having been killed on earth by a bus, developed such a fondness for the experience that he craved being knocked down weekly by a public passenger vehicle.

Now as everybody knows, Jamaican buses are willing to knock down a man in his prime of life if he clearly does not desire it. But let that same man request a knocking down for fun and see what he gets: bullheaded road courtesy and fanatical safe driving by every bus driver.

In heaven, however, the youth's wish was gladly granted, and every Saturday at noon an overloaded bus punctually careened around a corner and knocked him for a six into a goat pasture, after which he would joyfully leap to his feet and hurl the ripest cuss words at the driver, who sped away laughing.

That is heaven's way: no harm, hurt, sorrow or regret. All is joyful and fun—even being licked down by a bus.

I washed my face and prepared to open the shop, for now that Miss B was gone, I instinctively knew that I was clearly in charge, that the shop had become my responsibility, and that I had been led here in the first place because of my vast experience in retail management.

I sat down at a table in the back room and made notes of what I would do with the shop.

To begin with, I would throw away the charge book. From now on, everybody would pay for goods with cash money on the counter, not by signing a book.

I would immediately begin keeping two sets of accounts, one showing the right amount of money the shop had taken in every week, the other a bogus book intended for the government showing half the true amount. Being as I was in heaven and not hell, I saw no reason to depart from normal earth practice by keeping honest books and paying full tax.

So far I had not seen a tax collector and did not know if such a person existed in heaven. But I reasoned that with the government offering public services such as free pumpum caulking and hood removal for Christians, somebody had to pay for it, and Baps should not be the one to do so with his hard-earned money. If an incoming Christian wanted her pumpum caulked, that was her business, but such a service, in my humble opinion, should be privatised, not funded with taxpayers' dollars.

I decided, also, that to be a true Jamaican shop certain shortages and restrictions on the sale of goods had to be put into effect to be waived at the discretion of the proprietor. What was the fun of owning a shop if the shopkeeper wasn't in a position to make customers beg him to sell them goods?

I hand-lettered a sign announcing that no customer would be allowed to buy more than one pound of sugar per day.

There were other important matters that I needed to know about and on which Miss B had not enlightened me. For example, where would I buy goods? I had never seen a wholesale salesman, but obviously such a person must exist or the shelves would soon be bare.

I decided to take stock, to see what inventory I had on hand. I went into the shop and by the dawn light began a careful count of the tinned goods.

I was done with counting and, out of habit from my days on earth, felt to eat a tin of sardines for breakfast, although I was not hungry, for a heavenly belly always feels contentedly full.

There were three tins of sardines on the shelf. I removed one and carried it into the back room, intending to eat it at the table where I had been working.

I opened the tin and went back into the store for some harddough bread to squeegee up the oil on the plate.

It was then that I noticed that there were exactly three tins of sardines back on the shelf—the same number as before.

I stopped and looked and asked myself if I had miscounted. Puzzled, I took one of the tins off the shelf and left the room with it. When I returned a few minutes later, I discovered that another had materialised in its place.

No matter how many tins of sardines I took off the shelf, I always had three remaining.

As I stood there marvelling at this replenishment, I realised that this was why Miss B had been so careless with her stocktaking, because she never could run out of anything! This was why she didn't care about cash-and-carry—her goods cost her nothing!

Under the circumstances—controlling the only shop in the village and having no overhead plus an endless supply of free goods—I saw at once that the only sensible business move was to drastically mark-up prices and gouge the shopping public.

And that is what I did that first morning after Miss B's rebirth.

It was still early when I threw open the front doors to an empty coil of village street that glistened in the dawn wisps.

My first customer shuffled in around 8:30 a.m. to buy some sugar, still wearing the slightly frizzy look of a woman who had been lately abed. When she saw the sign announcing the rationing of sugar, she looked puzzled.

"Sugar short?" she asked, eyeing me suspiciously.

"Yes," I replied. "One pound per customer today."

"Sugar can't short in heaven, Mr. Baps. Nothing short up here."

"We have to practise shortage. De socialists from the seventies in Jamaica soon dead, and when dey reach heaven, sugar bound to short."

She rubbed her nose and sniffed.

"Missah Baps, if it wasn't for you, we up in heaven would forget 'bout de days on earth when sugar was short. We would just go along on our merry way knowing sugar can never short, and forget de times o' tribulation when sugar used to short."

"Mi dear, ma'am!"

"But you remind us, Missah Baps, dat sugar used to short, even though sugar can never short."

"Quite so. Dat is why we must prepare for shortage."

"I see you point, Missah Baps. Anyway, beg you to sell me two pound o' sugar."

I studied her long and hard before exercising due discretion.

"Since is you," I said, "I will make an exception," weighing out and wrapping the two pounds of sugar for her.

"Thank you, Missah Baps."

Grabbing hold of my collar and drawing me close to her face, she darted a look around at the empty shop and village street and in a whisper urged me never again to weaken and break the discipline of rationing I was attempting to impose, no matter how much ole negar bawled and wailed about it.

Then she went away, after duly lamenting that the murderers back on earth always seemed to be slaughtering the same trash week in and week out and wondering why they couldn't concentrate, once in a blue moon, on posting some of the better class of Jamaicans to heaven where they were sorely needed.

Happily babbling in this vein, she set off through the empty village street, furrowing a path through the swirling mists.

During that first day of exercising sole management over the shop, I waged war on and off with the ill-mannered public.

I kicked out malingering youths, ran the doorpost leaners off my veranda, and expelled all noisy quarrellers from the premises.

But the big row of the day was over my new policy of cash on the spot, and man and woman customers alike looked stunned when I told them flatly that all purchases must be paid for with real money.

"Money?" one woman gagged as if the word made her stifle. She shifted uncertainly in her tracks and stared at me as if her eyes had never before beheld a cash-and-carry shopkeeper. "What dat mean?"

"It mean dat from now on all is discipline and fiscal restraint."

"No more writing down in de book?"

"Precisely. Book day done."

A long pause pushed between us while she studied me.

Finally, she scowled and said that in that case she'd have to get some money, and she disappeared out of the shop and returned a few minutes later with a handful of crisp twenty-dollar bills.

Customer after customer did the same thing that long first morning, and I remained perplexed as to why the wretches were so determined to trust goods when they all obviously had bands of money.

It was only later that afternoon that I found out what was happening.

A boy had come into the shop to buy a sweetie and after handing me a new twenty-dollar bill, he shambled away nonchalantly.

"Hey, boy!" I called after him. "Take you change!"

He shrugged and said, "Oh," and came back in with his hand outstretched, looking sullen and uncaring.

"You almost walk off and leave de money!" I scolded. "Money don't grow on tree, you know."

His face lit up with a bright grin. "Money grow on tree, sah," he blurted with an ill-mannered giggle.

"Don't be impertinent, boy! Not because you in heaven I can't box you down."

"But, sah! A money tree right in you backyard!"

He pointed and headed out the front door towards the rear of my shop. I scurried around the counter and followed him—determined to teach the little wretch not to lie—and he led me to the fenced off backyard behind my shop and pointed to what I had mistaken for a breadfruit tree.

Swaying high up in its leafy crown was a middle-aged woman I had just run out of my shop because she had wanted to trust some goods. She was balancing on a branch and reaching out to pick twenty-dollar bills from a bunch that rustled and twirled in the afternoon breeze.

She clambered down the trunk unsteadily, for she was not dressed for tree climbing, brushed herself off, and disdainfully handed me a bunch of new bills.

"Dis is your idea of fiscal restraint?" I bellowed, stupefied at her gall. "To come pay me for my goods with money you pick off my backyard tree?"

She dusted off her skirt and said she didn't know anything about any fiscal restraint, but she had climbed the tree fair and square and picked the money and now please to give her the goods she wanted so she could go about her business.

"All morning de whole damn lot of you have been climbing my own tree and paying me with my own money!" I raged.

The youth giggled and gloated, "See! Money grow on tree!" and sauntered away with a triumphant swagger.

I hollered and bawled and raised the dickens and felt like a fool, but then I gave the woman her goods and she walked off in a peevish mood after turning to me and

growling spitefully, "One of dese fine days, Baps, I goin'
hold you down and grind you 'til you headtop drop off."

Ignoring her threat, I immediately made another sign
that blared, "NOTICE TO THE PUBLIC. PRIVATE
MONEY TREE! NO CLIMBING. NO FLYING. NO
PICKING. BY ORDER. TADDEUS BAPS, ESQ."

Tacking it to the money tree, I went back into my
shop feeling aggrieved that once again ole negar had
made me look like a monkey.

In the villages of heaven as in earth, what goes down
one woman's ear immediately pops out of another
woman's mouth, with the result that "discipline" and
"fiscal restraint" spread quickly among the population
like oldtime polio. Indeed, that very evening as I was
strolling through the peaceful countryside, some urchins
playing cricket in a field bawled out as I passed, "Missah
Fiscal Restraint!" and "Busha Discipline!", which
gladdened my spirits and made me walk with a brisker
step.

Breathing the fresh scents of the countryside, I
wandered over a footpath that wormed through the
greenery and encountered the white man whom I had
met earlier in the bush. He was squatting gloomily
against the trunk of a tree, playing in the dirt.

"Mr. Philosopher," I greeted him, "how you do?"

He shrugged. "To do you must first be."

"But you do be," I countered in a mischievous voice,
sitting down nearby on a stump and preparing for
bracing argument. "As a matter of fact, you *be* in the
Jamaican countryside. What you doin' here anyway?"

He looked puzzled. "I am not in the Jamaican
countryside," he finally said. "If I were, I'd be the first to
know it."

"But you are here! In the parish of St. Ann. Sitting under a Bombay mango tree."

He thought about what I had said. "Let me see what happened. I was sick. I died. I was quite sure that I died. I even heard the doctor say, 'He's dead.' But that was obviously from the fever, for if I were really dead, I'd be dead. Yet I know I am dead. So I can't be where you say I am. Where's that, by the way?"

"Jamaican bush. St. Ann parish."

"I must have flown here. I thought I was flying, saw a nice place to land and landed. But being dead, of course, I couldn't have done that. As I said, to do you must first be."

"And as I said, you do be."

"I do not be. Neither do you. I would be the first to know."

"So if you don't do, and I do not be, how come I'm sitting there talking to you and you're answering?"

He looked briefly puzzled before brightening. "Because you are in my head."

The brute didn't know where he was. He didn't even know how he got where he was but didn't think he was. Yet he was proposing a line of reasoning that had him, a visitor to my country, philosophically confining me, a Jamaican national, inside his tourist head. This kind of bamboozled thinking made my hackles rise.

I glared at him long and hard. "Please release me from your head, sah, or I'll have to tie you up."

"Why?"

"Because you might wander away and carry me off with you. So admit I not in your head or I going to tie you to a tree."

He rolled his eyes as if he couldn't understand my logic. Then, with a little gesture, he shrugged and said that every man must follow his own heart.

I grimly tore some creepers and vines off the ground and proceeded to lash him firmly to the trunk of the mango tree. I was prepared to knock the brute down if he resisted and, having thumped down many a hooligan in my day, I expected no trouble in coping with a puny white man. Fortunately for him, he put up no fight.

I strapped him to the tree, stepped back and admired my handiwork.

"Now, Mr. Philosopher," I declared smugly, "you are tied to a tree."

"I am not tied to anything. A man who is not, cannot be tied."

"We'll soon see whether shopkeeper 'knot' stronger dan philosopher 'not'," I laughed, strolling back to my shop in a cool and enjoyable evening breeze, leaving the brute tied to the tree like a rambunctious ramgoat.

Chapter 10

Two or three weeks had passed, and no man in heaven was more content than I, Taddeus Baps.

Discipline and fiscal restraint were catching on among the population, and I was even invited by a village parson to come and discuss money management with his congregation that following Sunday. He told me solemnly that just because money grew on trees up here did not mean that fiscal mismanagement must run amok among the baptised community, and he was sick and tired of the everlasting squandering of funds that even decent people carried on with, especially when the five-hundred dollar trees were in season.

I was very clearly making my mark in the village. People would occasionally stop me on my evening walks and congratulate me for bringing backbone and discipline to heaven, and not an evening passed when one or two good-neighbourly sisters didn't visit the shop to inquire if I might be in need of a healthful bedtime grind.

So I was definitely earning the respect of the public, even though I was a newcomer to the district, and I took pride in this accomplishment.

One day I decided to go on my evening stroll into that part of the bush where I had tied up the American philosopher, certain that I would not find him still hanging there, for in heaven even a hardened criminal bound with chains can escape by merely wishing freedom. However, if I did find him there, it would only prove that he was the biggest fool in heaven, and I felt in the mood to match wits with a complete idiot.

Whistling with joy, I was walking down the footpath to the clearing where I had left the philosopher when I heard the cracking sounds of stones being thrown and glimpsed a rowdy band of American youths standing next to an overgrown gully and pelting a towering tree with rocks. Nearby on the grass a village constable was dozing in spite of their noisy clatter.

Curious, I wandered over and asked one of the youths, who was rummaging the ground for a stone to throw, what they were doing. He panted that they were from a university in America and had come to Jamaica on a field trip.

At this, he let fly a rockstone at the crown of the tree with all his might.

"But who you stoning?" I asked, watching the rock whiz into the tree and ricochet with a loud crack off a fat limb.

"God!"

"Who?"

"God!" he barked gruffly, hurling another stone at the tree with a whoosh of effort. "God's in that tree."

After a paralysing stab of disbelief and shock, I grabbed the youth by the shoulders and pitched him headlong down the gully as he was in the act of throwing.

"Hey!" he screamed as he went flying.

"What'd you do that for, you old Jamaican fart?" another youth screeched, charging me.

I grabbed the little wretch by the neck, gave it a wring, and tossed him atop the napping constable, who sprang to his feet with an astonished roar, hurling the boy off him.

A free-for-all followed, with six American youths ganging up on me, and some vicious freewheeling thumping was exchanged.

Of course, thumping in heaven being sweet both to thumper and thumped, the scuffle only caused all of us to split our sides with delight before the noisy hubbub brought the boys' professor crashing through the bush and demanding to know who had started the fight.

"As long as I have strength and breath," I stormed, "I'll thump down any man or boy who dare stone my God!"

A scornful hiss swelled from the milling students, and the professor had to shout to quiet them down.

"They are angry with God," he announced calmly, "for destroying Hypsilophodon, exterminating Brontosaurus, wiping out the entire line of Tyrannosaurus Rex."

"He didn't even leave a single Pteranodon behind," one of the students moaned sorrowfully, as if he was talking about his murdered grandmother.

In the uneasy silence that settled over the bushland, I turned to the constable and asked him if he knew what these demented foreigners were talking about.

He muttered that he was sorry, he didn't know, but these names sounded to him like the street nicknames of certain vicious Kingston gunmen.

"We're talking about dinosaurs," the professor explained in a voice that said he was addressing an idiot. "These were all dinosaur species that God wiped out."

"Dinosaurs!" I exploded. "You stone God because He clean de earth of a few nasty lizard?"

The students roared indignantly in one voice, surging to flail at me, but the professor bellowed above the tumult at them to shut up.

As the rumble died down, one of the sullen youths muttered, "Ignorant Jamaican," loud enough for me to hear. I lunged into the crowd and thumped him right on his top lip, causing him to squeal with ecstasy, and the professor had to restrain the others from charging me and inflicting the joys of pummelling on my person.

"Listen, you, whatever your name is," the professor cried, his eyes afire, "let's ask God if what I say isn't true."

He shouted at the tree growing in the gully, "God, didn't you make Hypsilophodon extinct?"

An ominous pause followed as we all waited expectantly and stared at the thicket of the tree. A breeze riffled through the clearing and a musically polite voice answered, It wasn't that simple.

For the benefit of those readers who have never conversed with the Almighty, let me add a brief word of explanation about God talk.

In Hollywood movies God talks in peals of thunder and bolts of lightning. In heaven, however, God talks only in thoughts. All the religious cavorting that goes on at Revival meetings where worshippers will shriek and roll on the ground and babble and claim that God is talking in tongues through them, is never God; it's duppy encyclopaedia salesmen from America, who like to hang around Revival tent poles for a joke and babble through the so-called possessed.

"What'd you mean, 'It wasn't that simple?' Under your stewardship, didn't Diplodocus, Pteranodon and Tyrannosaurus Rex, and all the other dinosaurs become extinct?" the professor asked while barbing me with an accusing stare.

Again a lofty and breezy pause followed by the same soft voice, I suppose so.

"Murderer!" yelled one of the students, his face turning red with fury.

I reached over to box the boy's nasty mouth but the constable held me back. "Mr. Baps, don't be so hot-tempered."

"We're anthropology students from Harvard," the professor explained. "How do you expect us to feel?"

"I don't care a damn where you come from," I raged in his face, "and I don't care what you feel. Dis is God Almighty you dealing with. Show some respect."

"Respect for someone who wiped out a whole animal species?" muttered one of the students darkly.

The argument raged back and forth in the clearing. I stood my ground and swore that anytime my eye saw a foreigner stoning my God on the soil of Jamaica, all hell would pop, for I would smite jaw and nose and face without mercy, adding that I didn't understand why Almighty God didn't just use His everlasting powers and turn the whole lot of them into fish bait.

At this remark, the youths exploded in an uproarious laughing and staggered away down the trail, periodically collapsing against each other with uncontrollable mirth as if they had never before heard a bigger joke. The constable trailed sheepishly after them, mumbling apologetically over his shoulder that American youth were known universally to be unruly.

After they had gone I asked God if He was all right, and He answered Yes. I asked Him if His feelings were hurt by the disrespect shown and He said, Not really.

The conversation languished for a bit as I stared hard at the thick leaves of the tree and tried to spot God.

"Well," I said lamely, "I was on me way to debate a philosopher I tied to a tree. So I suppose I better go."

I paused, gave the tree another searching look, and was about to head down the trail when I impulsively asked God if He would like to come with me and visit the tied up philosopher.

"Dat is," I added, not wanting to seem as if I were pushing myself up on Him, "if he's still tied and if you not too busy."

He said, No, He was not at all busy, and He would like to come and see for Himself which philosopher I had tied up and find out why.

Then God flew out of the tree and hovered in the clearing not three feet from where I, Taddeus Baps, stood, stupefied and overjoyed at meeting face to face with my Maker.

Chapter 11

God looks like a peenywally.

He is a tiny bubble of the purest starlight, and when He first darted out of the crown of the tree and hovered near my face, I might have mistaken Him for a flickering peenywally—what some people call a firefly or lightning bug—except that His glitter was so blinding. It was a shock at first, to see that God was so small, for my upbringing had led me to expect a big and powerful Somebody with meat on the bone and plenty muscle.

"God, is dat you?" I asked, nervous and uncertain, knowing that I was not good enough in heart and mind to come face to face with the Almighty, for my love of moneymaking and craving for earthly pumpum had led me over the years to double deal and connive, but that's another story and will not be disclosed in these pages on the advice of barrister.

It is enough for me to say that I knew myself to be an unrepentant sinner and unworthy to be in the presence of the Almighty.

He said, How do you do, Baps?

I replied that I was well—thank you—adding that I very much liked the runnings of heaven, and He replied that He wished the Americans did, too, but they were always giving Him a hard time and trying to get Him to change up heaven.

I advised him not to pay them any mind, for they didn't have any sense.

He chuckled and said, That was a refreshing attitude to have, and He would remember it the next time he was stoned by a class from Harvard.

"Just call on me, God! I'll thump down de brutes for You!"

He said, Thank you very much, Baps, but He didn't too much relish fisticuffs or pugilism.

"Den I'll bring me machete and chop dem up, for dey is out of order to stone Almighty God."

He said that He appreciated my willingness to fight on His behalf but He didn't really care for cleaving, chopping, decapitation, or any other form of butchery, either.

"You a hard man to please, sah!" I said jokingly, then apologised quickly, thinking that I had spoken disrespectfully. But God only laughed, and His laughter sounded so sweet that throughout my friendship with Him I was constantly peppering Him with clean jokes just to hear that joyful sound.

Of course, being a wretch, I know mainly dirty joke, and it was always a serious strain to keep my humour wholesome.

We had started down the trail, God flying near my right shoulder, a drop of the loveliest light quivering in a sparkling bubble no bigger than a teardrop. As we trekked I exulted to myself, 'Baps, you lucky son of a gun! Imagine, you, a humble, dirty-minded, lowdown shopkeeper, and here God is flying beside your earhole and chatting with you as if the two of you were best friend.'

My indoor parson, however, grumbled, "Dis peenywally is God? Where de golden throne? Where de cherub? Where de hosts bawling hosanna? Where you see even one angel, one seraph, one principality, even one fool-fool power? Dis peenywally can't be God!"

"Hush up you mouth and show respect!" I hissed.

God asked me if I had said something.

I said, No, I was talking to my parson.

What parson? God wondered. Was there a parson lurking in the pathway bush?

I had never before in my life admitted to anyone that a parson dwelled inside me, but this was God Almighty I was talking to, and thinking that there was no concealing anything from His eyes, I told Him the whole story about how I had come to the longtime habit of self-preaching that had over the years petrified into an indoor parson. I added that the problem with an indoor parson is that you can't thump him down without also thumping down yourself, as you could an outdoor parson, and He recommended that I try exorcism.

"Exorcise who?" my parson bellowed angrily. "You don't exorcise a man o' de cloth!"

"Hush up!"

The bubble of light glittered as merrily as a Christmas sparkler, which meant that the spirit of the Almighty was laughing in the Kingdom of Heaven.

We trudged the rest of the way to the clearing in silence.

When we got to the tree I found to my astonishment that the philosopher, looking somewhat bedraggled and bored, still dangled from the tree where I had left him.

Fearing that God would be vexed with me, I hastened to untie the fellow, asking him in a furtive undertone, "Why you didn't just leave, man?"

The stubborn wretch looked me up and down and said, "Leave, where?"

"Here, idiot!" I whispered, struggling with my own knots. "You didn't have to remain tied. You could've just walked away!"

"A man has to be before he can walk."

"Shut up 'bout dat same stupid old story! Be thankful you in heaven. And see, here's God, come to look for you!"

Swivelling his head and focusing his bleary eyes towards the glittering drop of light hovering next to his shoulder, the philosopher jumped like he had been struck by lightning.

"It is God!" he yelped.

"You better tie him up back to de tree," my parson muttered surlily. "De man is stark, raving mad!"

I really can't say I was comfortable that first evening I spent in the company of God. Indeed, I sat in the clearing as the evening light sifted through the surrounding grove of trees spattering leafy patterns on the ground and blurted out to God that I was a wretch, a nasty, conniving backbiter who wasn't worthy to be in His presence.

"You right 'bout dat!" my parson hissed.

God wondered why I felt so about myself when from all He could see I was quite a decent chap.

"Because I loved pumpum too gluttonously when I was on earth, Oh, Lord," I quavered in a craven voice. "I used to chase it all de time, and when a maid wouldn't give me, sometimes..." here my lips trembled with contrition and my voice cracked, "sometimes I would fire her, for I am a wicked, no-good brute."

I was going to add that of late some of these maids from the country were meaner with the pumpum than a dog with a bone and well deserved firing, but I held myself in check by remembering that no earthly excuse could atone for my wanton behaviour.

Perched like a bird on the low-lying branch of a tree, God seemed to digest this candid confession with some gravity.

Finally, he wondered in a bemused voice what was pumpum.

"What is pumpum? Lord, it's what you always blasting in scripture!"

God said that I must be mistaken, for He had nothing at all against pumpum, and whether I felt like chasing it or butterfly was my business.

I had to laugh at this naiveté.

"Oh, pumpum much harder to catch dan butterfly, Lord," I said in worldly explanation, adding, "but to say you have nothing 'gainst pumpum after everything you write 'bout it...."

I never wrote a word about it, God declared firmly.

"Den who write all those harsh words 'gainst pumpum?"

God thought for a brief moment or so and said that he didn't really know but that a long time ago there was a bearded chap who had been bucked off a horse someplace in the Middle East—He couldn't exactly remember when or where—and hit his head on a rockstone, and when the fellow woke up he began railing against something similar, although he didn't call it pumpum, which must be a Jamaican nickname....Hmmm....What did he call it again?

"You talking 'bout St. Paul on de road to Damascus!" my parson bellowed with outrage. "Dat is blasphemy!"

He remembered now, God recalled dreamily. The fellow who dropped off the horse and hit his head got up screeching against women.

"Some people call it dat," I said gloomily.

The philosopher jumped to his feet and took an erratic spin around the stout trunk of a nearby tree, looking bewildered and lost in thought. A few minutes later he sat back down with a satisfied smirk.

"What sweet you?" I asked him.

"The sight of God shook me up and made me question my theory about oblivion after death. But I see now that there's a simple explanation."

"What dat?"

"God must be in my head, too, along with everything else. Now, if you don't mind disappearing for a bit, I'm going to take a walk and think this through."

With that, he wandered away down the trail, glancing once over his shoulder to see if we were disappearing before he was swallowed up in the bush.

"If dis peenywally is truly God," my parson shrieked in his harshest brimstone voice, "why he didn't smite those rude American students, eh? Why?"

Chapter 12

I am not a pushy man: I don't rub up to big shot politician just to pepper them with questions on their days off. But I had plenty questions to ask God.

For example, why was excursion bus and boat and train rammed with ole negar always crashing, sinking, and derailing, resulting in ole negar breaking neck, drowning, and being blown to smithereens by the dozen? Why every time a ferry sank in some woebegone foreign land it was always crammed with pure ole negar? And how come every time I read about a crocodile or a tiger or a lion in some misbegotten country devouring someone, it was always a ole negar being eaten? How come white man never get eaten, too, or does he taste too bad?

Naturally, I have also always wondered what made woman so hardheaded and tough, but out of respect I didn't want to clean bowl the Almighty with my opening ball.

Still, I was hesitant to discuss politics with the Lord, and that first evening in the bush we mainly chatted about current events and sports and all kind of horse dead and cow fat.

Later, we strolled through the countryside—at least I walked while God flew next to my ear. The evening was lovely with a freshening breeze, and soon the philosopher melted out of the bush and fell in step beside me and demanded of God to know certain truths about the beginning of the universe.

God said He personally had no beginning, that there was never a day when He didn't exist, at which point the philosopher asked in a quarrelsome tone how that could be when everything had a beginning.

God replied that the philosopher had been bamboozled by the clock. Before He created time, God explained, there was no such thing as beginning and end, start and stop, sooner and later, arrive and depart, now and then, and past and present. There was only was was or was was not. He was was. Everything else was was not.

"So," I clarified, feeling a little giddy and philosophical meself in the evening breeze, "was was or was was not was all dere was?"

That's exactly right, God nodded.

"So, for instance, dere was no dog, no puss, no rat, and no mongoose?"

No.

"No stepladder, no bus, no thief and no petty cash pan?"

No.

"No domino, no sugar bun, no pum....I mean, no pineapple or pomegranate?"

"This is rubbish!" the philosopher snapped. "Shut up with the endless particulars and let Him talk."

"You want me to thump down you backside in de bush right now? Come tell me to shut up like I'm a bwoy! You think you can keep shop and deal with ole negar all dese years and not feel philosophical now and again?"

God cut in and said that sometimes He wished He'd followed His mind and created a clockless universe where everything happened at once like in the booths at a garden party.

"Well, God," I declared, speaking from bitter experience, "is a good thing You didn't do dat, for knowing de earthly sisters like I do, dere's no way dey going jump up in church and give out pumpum at de same time. Whereupon all grinding would therefore cease and de whole population perish."

"I still don't understand why You created the universe," the philosopher said sourly.

God tried to explain creation in a way we could understand.

He said that in this beginning He was an immensity and alone in a warm swirling broth of darkness. There was no sun; there was no world, no moon, no stars; there was nothing but His immensity in an ocean of terrible darkness; and when He shifted or turned the darkness lapped against and tickled a cranny of His being that, for the sake of argument, we could call His armpits.

One day, He said, during a moment of monstrous tickling, He got fed up and bawled out in the infinite blackness, "Let there be stick!"

We swished single-file through the bush in deep silence, digesting this vivid first moment of creation.

The philosopher broke the awed stillness by barking, "Stick? Your first creation was stick?"

Yes.

"But God," I protested, "dis is not what we learn in Bible school. You didn't say 'Let dere be light'?"

God said, But wait! Baps, you know you Bible!

"I had a wicked aunt who used to beat de Old Testament into me," I muttered. "She made me memorise almost de whole o' it, and she brooked no error or worldly interpretation. One time I make de mistake and say to her, 'Dese people in de Old Testament were a hard breed o' people: either dey knewing one anodder or dey slewing one anodder,' and she nearly kill me with a tamarind switch. When it come to her Bible, she was a hard woman, God. And she say dat you say, 'Let dere be light!' and dere was light."

God said He said, Let there be stick. And there was stick.

"Den what after stick?"

Scratching with the stick.

I said, "Oh, first stick, den scratching. Make sense. Den what next?"

He said, then leaf, for the stick looked scrawny and ugly without a leaf.

"First stick, den leaf?" I asked, making sure I got the sequence right. "When did de light come?"

God said light came later, that He didn't create the universe from the top down, but from the bottom up, no matter what you read. Stick was first. Light was last.

We were trampling through the bush path as we talked, and I began to feel like I got all that bust-assing over the years for nothing, and I griped to God how come He let me Auntie nearly kill me with beating to memorise de Bible when de whole book was wrong? All dat beating over the years, for what? To memorise a stinking lie?

"And you know what else?" I groused. "If I could buck her up now and tell her how it really go—dat You say You create stick first—she'd bust me head and make me repent. Dis is not a fair life, you know, God? Man not supposed to get beating because him don't memorise a lie."

God said that I had a point, but He never told my Auntie to beat me.

"But she beat me in Your name!" I bawled.

But without proper authorisation, He said.

We plodded deeper into the bush, our feet cracking twigs underfoot.

"I should go look her up and thump her down!"

God said, Baps, you wouldn't do that to you old Auntie. You are too much the gentleman.

"Gentleman, me back foot, God!" I squawked. "Is not one beating she give me over dis damn Bible, you know? Is not two beating! Is not even twenty or thirty beating! Is at least one hundred backside beating! She'd say, 'And Cain knew his wife and she bore him who?' and if you didn't bawl out 'Enoch' right away, you'd get a bitch lick. And den she'd say, 'And Seth live a hundred and five years, and he beget who?' and if you didn't bawl out, 'Enosh, with a 's', buuf! anodder bitch lick! And woe be unto you backside if you ever mix up 'Enoch' wid 'Enosh!' Buuf! Buuf! Buuf! Buuf! Bitch lick fall like rain!"

God said He knew that bitch lick was painful on earth, but didn't it feel wonderful in heaven?

I sputtered, "Yes, of course! But is on earth dat aunties love to drop bitch lick on boy pickney! Come up here when dem know a lick sweet, you think dem goin' drop even one? Dem would-a dead first!"

I must admit that I was feeling sore-hearted about the recollection, but not unhappy, because no heart can feel unhappiness in heaven even when it's miserable.

The philosopher suddenly stopped in his tracks, dropped on the ground, tore off his right shoe and popped a nasty wet kiss on his own big toe. "My Lord and my God!" he croaked.

"What now?" I asked suspiciously.

"I must be God! I didn't realise it until just now! It just hit me! Please leave, so I can worship me."

"You want me to kick you backside all over dis field?"

God sparkled with laughter and said, Come Baps, let's continue on our way.

"But dis damn man say dat he's God! He need a good lick!"

But God just chuckled and continued down the path, and when I turned to look just before we crested a ridge and descended into a wavy lowland pasture, I saw that the philosopher had grabbed a religious fanatic petchary off a nearby limb to fire up as a burnt offering to himself while the zealous bird tweeted with evangelical hysteria, "Singe me backside! Burn me in de righteous fire! Scald me unholy rass in de heavenly pot!"

From that first meeting on, God and me walked the countryside of heaven as close personal friends.

No doubt some readers are asking why Almighty God would develop a friendship with a wretch like me, and to tell the truth, I used to wonder about that myself in the beginning. The only explanation I can give is that I never made a fuss over Him, thinking that over the years He had probably had His bellyful of worship and adoration.

"Baps," I asked myself that night after our first meeting as I lay abed listening to a patoo outside my window, "how would you feel if you were God Almighty and de multitudes were forever bawling praise and glory in you name morning noon and night?"

I thought long and hard about it in the darkness of the room before whispering a heartfelt reply, "Ole negar bawling hallelujah over me instead of shoplifting? Who could ask for more?"

Thinking deeper on the subject, however, I saw at once that God Almighty must be sick and tired of all the hymning and fussing over Him and probably wanted nothing more than to be treated just like another customer.

So I never jumped up in His presence like I was at a revival meeting; I never hosannahed; and the nearest I ever came to expressing worship was once, the second time we met, when I gave Him a friendly clap, which made His stardust splatter.

From that day forth God and me were as close as batty and bench.

Chapter 13

For the next few weeks God and me gallivanted all over the countryside. We went to cricket match, agricultural fair, and hiked up mountain trails where we would bawl "moo" to cows grazing on hillside pastures, making them jump while we scampered off, laughing wildly. We trekked down to rivers for a swim in cool bubbling water while janga shrimp peered out suspiciously at us from the shadows of overhanging water reeds. A nicer, more good-natured companion than God a man can never have, and He and I romped during those fun-filled days over the countryside of heaven as carefree as schoolboys on summer holiday.

That was when I began to notice that American tourists were always going out of their way to attack and try to kidnap God.

One day, for example, as we were coming from the river, an American Baptist minister jumped out of the bush and swatted at God with a fish net. I dropped the wretch with a good thump that made him squeal with ecstasy, and we grappled and rolled down the gorge, fighting and biting and shivering with the joy of thump. We ended up sprawled on the river bank, muddy water trickling over our clothes as we strangled each other, enjoying mutual suffocation while God soared over the fray and sparkled at our delight.

The Baptist jumped up and bellowed crossly that he hated fighting in heaven where a thump felt sweet, he couldn't stand that shooting and knifing were all wholesome family values, and as far as he was concerned heaven was a demented and unholy land for which God was to blame.

But even as he said this he was chortling, for no man in heaven can be unhappy, and frustration only makes the malcontent happier.

Another time me and God were in the middle of administering a domino six-love in the side yard of my shop when two American Junior Chamber of Commerce leaders rushed through the gate and tried to chop up God with a machete, hacking so wildly that they slashed off the foot of a bystander who loafed nearby criticising the play.

This being heaven, the severed limb immediately sprang back like a frisky frog and reattached itself to the body, occasioning no bodily harm and tickling the victim.

The rest of us grabbed the brutes and beat them so hard that they begged us not to stop. They swore afterwards that the experience of a Jamaican village beating was more delightful than being hanged last year for spitting on a street in Singapore. From now on, they vowed, as we threw them out onto the street, they would spread the word to their friends about the wonders of a Jamaican lick.

In a third episode, two American Bible students hid themselves in a tree overhanging the footpath leading to the river and tried to drop a grocery bag over God as He flew past. I pulled them off the limb and gave them such a satisfying kick that they immediately bent over and begged a second helping.

When I asked the wretches why Americans were always trying to capture Almighty God, they explained breathlessly that there was a Federal bounty on Him, and if they had succeeded in bringing Him back for the authorities, they would have been national heroes.

"We'd even have gotten extra credit in our Homiletics class, too," one said, looking disappointed. "And a definite 'A.'"

"Get an 'A' by doing you lessons and studying hard," I scolded, "not by trying to unlawfully capture de Almighty."

"But God is wanted in every state!" one of the youths protested.

"He's a fugitive from justice!"

"He's on the run from the Feds!"

"You still can't come here and think to capture God without getting a bitch lick from patriotic Jamaicans. Now go 'bout you business and leave de Almighty alone."

They turned, shuffled partway down the woodland trail, paused, and hurried back looking hopeful.

"Do you think you could drop kick me again?" one of them asked.

"Me, too," the other seconded. "That was the most fun."

"No. I don't drop kick tourists. Dat is harassment."

"We don't mind being harassed!"

"I said no! Idle brutes! Go 'bout you business!"

Why was Almighty God wanted in America? What law did He break, and how dare the American government encourage its citizens to travel to Jamaica and try to capture the creator?

I asked God one day after we'd enjoyed a brisk river swim and were sitting on the banks sunning ourselves but He shrugged and said there were basic differences between Him and the Americans, that they had sent umpteen delegations to Him, arguing that a hell was needed, that common decency demanded celestial pain and suffering.

"Pain and suffering?" I asked, amazed. "Dey want you to put pain and suffering in heaven?"

Yes, God said, and they were quite dogmatic about it, too. They wanted to hang a criminal and make him stay hanged, with a broken neck that hurt like the dickens even in the afterlife. They wanted bombing that would make the bombees bawl bloody murder. They especially hated the three universal laws of heaven.

I asked God please to explain these universal laws.

He numbered them for me, and I write them down in the exact words of the Almighty's thoughts that flowed into my brain that afternoon on the river bank.

Law 1: Water shalt find its own level.

Law 2: Thou shalt feel good no matter what.

Law 3: Thou cannot capture the Lord thy God.

After the Almighty was finished, I asked for clarification of meaning.

"What it mean dat water find its own level?"

God replied that if thou was a wretch, a low-down thief, a nasty and unrepentant dog, thou wouldst find other thief and dog of thy bosom to cleave to and keep thy company in heaven and wouldst not have to consort with well-spoken clerks and sanctimonious churchgoers while pining for the companionship of other dirty-minded thief and dog.

"So dog and thief can walk together and make each odder happy. Hallelujah! Give praise! What law two mean?"

That law, God said, meant that no matter what thou doest in heaven, whether thou shouldst buck thy toe on a rockstone or fall off a mountain top and break thy neck, thou wouldst find the experience sweet, wouldst feel no pain, ache, injury, hurt, discomfort or twinge in thy bones, for thou wouldst be always blessedly happy in heaven.

I digested for a moment the meaning of this powerful law, for it explained why even a busted head in heaven was pure bliss and delight.

"And law three?"

That one was easy, said God, for it meant that thou couldst move heaven and earth with thy science and industry, but no matter what thou didst, thou wouldst not be able to capture, lay hands on, extradite, or repatriate thy lord thy God, no matter whether thou tried obeah or butterfly net—thy God was immune to thy perversions of capture.

"God," I asked, after a long moment of ingestion and digestion, "how come you talking so funny?"

God laughed and asked if He was putting on an American twang. I said, No, He didn't have a twang, but He was 'thying' and 'thouing' and 'theeing' up the whole place.

He said He was sorry, but whenever He talked religion 'thou' and 'thy' and 'thee' jumped automatically into His mouth because of all the years of listening to Baptists and Holy Rollers.

"God," I joked, "thou hast an impressionable heart."

Baps, God replied chuckling, thy backside!

And the two of us burst out laughing so loud that a bullfrog sitting on the banks of the river gaped at us as if to ask if we took life for a joke.

I decided to further investigate the dispute between **God and the Americans.**

One afternoon I closed up my shop and took a walk to the village library and looked up back issues of the *Daily Gleaner* for stories about the quarrel with God.

I found out that God had resided in Jamaica for many years and had even become a naturalised citizen; that over the years the Americans had repeatedly pressed for His extradition to face charges on contempt of Congress for maliciously creating and obstinately maintaining an un-American heaven and had even given a deadline for raining down hydrogen bombs on the island if their demands about God continued to be ignored.

· I read that parliament had declared a national holiday on the anticipated day of the nuclear bombardment, with banks and insurance companies shutting down for the long weekend so that staff and their families could fully enjoy the anticipated holocaust. Enterprising vendors had printed tee-shirts with colourful logos and designs celebrating the occasion. Schools had closed islandwide for the week as they do during Easter so that pupils and faculty alike could have time off to relish Armageddon. The island's betting shops had posted odds on which parish would receive the first bomb, which the highest recorded megatonnage, which suffer the greatest radiation fallout.

I continued to read eagerly.

According to the *Gleaner*, on the day of the anticipated bombardment, all Jamaican public beaches, rivers, and picnic grounds were jammed to capacity with colourful masses of festive people winding up their bodies to the throbbing rhythms of reggae and soca as they eagerly awaited the joys of being blown to bits courtesy of the United States. Bickering and squabbling reportedly broke out among some of the celebrants who were diehard supporters of the Marine Corps and those who were staunch backers of the Air Force about which branch of the service could be expected to drop the sweetest bomb. A melee erupted between these rival factions at Dunns River, with rockstones and bottles pelting down on the heads of the teeming throng, busting skulls to the delight of the squealing, carousing revellers.

The *Gleaner* issue of that eagerly awaited day when the bombs were expected to fall ran erudite editorials and discussions about whether the hydrogen or the atomic bomb would be zestier to the unknowing Jamaican populace who were amateurs when it came to appreciating the finer points of bombardment. One columnist grumbled that dropping a hydrogen bomb on a Jamaican was casting pearls before swine, for the brute would be just as happy if you busted his skull with a pickaxe. Various connoisseurs weighed in with opinions that pooh-poohed the other side while stoutly arguing for the superiority of their favourite explosives.

The same *Gleaner* issue also contained full-page ads of appreciation to the Americans for the expected assault paid for by civic minded businesses, many of the ads featuring patriotic rhymes about the glories of America written by the winner of an islandwide poetry contest. Only the dreary Seventh Day Adventist churches in Jamaica had refused to participate in the national orgy, the *Gleaner* reported, threatening their members who partook of the bombing jamboree with expulsion.

I read one story after another and trembled, turning the pages as fast as I could read to see what had happened.

I found out that on the day when fire and destruction were expected to rain down on the innocent and fun-loving Jamaican merrymakers, nothing happened: the Republicans in the American Senate mounted a filibuster against the bombardment, claiming that it would only make the Federal deficit worse. Not a single drop of a bomb fell.

The frantic Jamaican government, seeing that throngs and hordes at the beaches and picnic grounds would be crushed with disappointment, ordered the Jamaican Defence Force to overfly the crowds and blast them with all available stores of Public Works Department dynamite. Police were ordered to compensate for the lack of entertainment by shooting excursion riders and revellers on sight until ammunition was exhausted and after that to run over as many as was practicable with their patrol cars. Throughout the island the dismay and disgust at the false alarm was so widespread that the temporary American ambassador was dragged out of his residence by rioters and hanged over and over again, much to his immense pleasure, causing him to telegraph Washington with the request that he be permanently posted to the island. Only the Seventh Day Adventists gloated, rebuking the population about reliance on fly-by-night bombing instead of looking to the Biblical promise of flood.

After that day of national disappointment, the *Gleaner* ran stories about the subsequent stormy meetings of parliament during which the government and opposition took turns blasting the Americans for their selfishness, with one member asking rhetorically, "Mr. Speaker, is this the act of a friend, an ally, to promise a bombing and then, for the sake of saving pennies, disappoint an entire nation?" at which the berobed speaker glowered and looked severe.

When I was done with my reading, I found that I was sweating with such excitement that I had to get some fresh air.

As I was walking out of the building I stopped off at the reception desk and asked the bespectacled librarian if she had been in heaven during the episode of the bogus bombing, which made her scowl disagreeably and grumble, "Baps, if you please, I don't want to talk about dat distressing day. I had a picnic lunch packed and me whole Sunday school class with me. De children were all excited 'bout de awaited bombing. Den come to tell, not even a firecracker fall, much less a bomb."

"Sorry."

"Well, what was was, and what is is, and what will be will be. You getting plenty grind, Baps?"

"Oh, yes. Plenty."

"We're all good Jamaican Christians, and we must be charitable in our hearts and grind one another regularly. None should lack pumpum in heaven. If de sisters neglecting you, even though I busy wid me grandchildren, I'll come grind you tonight."

"I grind enough already, ma'am."

"Since Miss B gone back down, I don't see you again in church. You backsliding?"

"Yes, ma'am. But I am seeking reform."

"Seek de said reform, Baps. Come back to us! Don't hang out with rude boy! And stop running around with God in de bush, bawling 'boo' at idle old cow. If dis wasn't heaven, de poor cow would already dead of heart failure."

"Yes, ma'am. Good evening."

"Good evening, Baps! Get grind regular. Uphold standards. Being in heaven don't mean dat slackness must triumph."

"No, ma'am."

With her kindly pieties still fresh in my ears, I ambled out into the village streets which were shimmering in the loveliness of another beautiful heavenly sunset.

Chapter 14

I am a curious man. I like to learn about the world and the people who inhabit it. Before I dropped dead, my hobby was studying geography books, especially memorising the names of mountains and rivers in the Temperate Zone.

So now that I was in heaven, I was eager to travel to other countries and was especially curious to visit the United States and find out why its people were so discontented with God.

One day as I was sitting behind the counter daydreaming about a trip abroad, I glimpsed Hopeton trudging up the hillside with another newly dead Jamaican in tow. I hurried into the back room and got out the official government register and re-entered the shop just as the guide and his duppy passenger walked through the front door.

The duppy turned out to be Hector, my thiefing gardener, who had just broken his neck by falling out of my mango tree.

We had a terrible blow-up then and there, for I was still peeved about how he and Mabel had stripped my wallet clean as soon as I was dead.

"Leap year bonus?" I raged at him. "You stinking dog!"

"Is Mabel make me do it, sah!" he whimpered.

Hopeton leaned against the counter and grinned during the whole row, but finally I registered the wretch of a gardener and the guide disappeared down into the bush path.

A lady from the village who had stopped by to pick up some flour offered to break-in Hector with a grind of welcome, and the two of them waddled across the street and disappeared down a gully.

A few hours later, the gardener staggered into my shop, did a dance and chuckled, "Dat nice lady give me seven grind 'pon de gully floor! I shoulda dead fifty year ago."

An idea was cooking in my brain. While it cooked, I stared up at him long and hard until he flinched. Finally, I asked him bluntly, "You want a work?"

He looked me over cagily.

"Work in heaven, sah? Man suppose to work up here? What kind of work?"

What I had in mind was training him to run my business while I went away on my trip. And the techniques of proper shopkeeping were what I intended to teach him—how to run a respectable shop that exerted rulership and discipline over ole negar.

Of course, I knew it wouldn't be easy, that I would have to slave like a dog to explain my philosophy of business, to demonstrate that we were not just keeping shop and selling goods, we were setting high moral tone and fostering discipline.

"Discipline, sah?" he seemed stunned at this far-reaching concept of shopkeeping. "We not just out to sell saltfish and flour?"

"On one level, we selling saltfish and flour. But on anodder level we ruling ole negar."

He held his head and wailed, "Lawd, Missah Baps, dis too deep for me poor brain, sah!"

"Dis is heaven, man! If you want a deeper brain, we can fill out a form and get you a deeper brain."

"I do plan to fill out a form, sah, and make de journey to Kingston for bodily improvement!"

I glared at him. "You want a bigger hood, right?"

He squirmed and looked embarrassed. "Missah Baps, what a way you can see right inna man heart!"

"You not even in heaven a day and already you taking de low road!"

"Dat road not low, Missah Baps! Dat road high, sah! Well high!"

"High? Arrive in heaven today, and right away you looking bigger hood at government expense. Dat is a high road?"

Our conversation was interrupted by the entrance of a regular customer—a matronly lady who resided in one of the settlements surrounding the village—and I took pains to serve her with every consideration and courtesy so that Hector could observe my philosophy of business in practice.

We exchange polite pleasantries about the weather and happenings in the community, and she purchased flour and salt and a pint of red peas, which she declared she intended to use in a soup for her husband's dinner.

She was gathering her things in a housewifely bustle to depart the premises when Hector mumbled, "Woe! I just reach heaven, not three hour gone!"

"Oh, yes?" she replied, beaming hospitably at him. "I hope one of de village ladies gave you a welcoming grind?"

I interrupted gruffly. "Him just get up off de gully ground."

"Just a tups," the liar muttered, slumping his shoulders and pretending to be wasting away.

"Dat is not satisfactory," the woman said decisively, piling her packages firmly atop the counter. "A newcomer deserve more grind dan a tups!"

"Me say de man just get up offa gully ground, Miss Lindsay! Him get seven grind inna row."

"Hi, Missah Baps!" Hector whispered frantically. "Have a heart, sah! I only just dead!"

"Now, Baps! Be Christian! Dis is a stranger among us!"

Arm-in-arm, the two of them trooped out of my shop and headed across the street towards the gully.

An hour later they returned beaming happily, and after the customer had finally left, Hector looked up at the ceiling of my shop and bellowed, "Heaven is one powerful location, sah!"

That week I told God about my plans to visit America, and He said He would like to accompany me.

We had gone on our usual stroll and were sitting in the grassy clearing when I brought up the subject. The American philosopher, who had been dogging our tracks all evening, grumbled that he didn't particularly wish to travel.

"You not invited," I told him bluntly.

"But if you go, I'll have to go, too," he snapped. "That's the nuisance about having you both inside my head."

"Stay home. We'll manage."

I frankly advised God against making the trip. I pointed out the dangers of mob violence, military action, impoundment and Kangaroo Court, telling him that a nation prepared to reward tourists for attempting capture and extradition of His person would stop at nothing should He attempt a forcible landing on their soil, but the Almighty laughed and said that I was forgetting the law of heaven which reads, "Thou cannot capture the Lord thy God."

"I don't forget. But dis is mob rule. Dese people hate your heaven. And dey are born lynchers."

God said nobody could lynch Him.

"So dey'd lynch me, den. For I hear dey don't like black people, either."

God asked if I wouldn't appreciate the joy of being lynched, and I replied, yes, a lynching would be a nice treat on my holiday, but still I wondered if it would be worth all the clamour and noise and babble.

God thought about it, sparkling near the limb of a tree under which we sat, and then He said He had an idea, how about if He went with me to America in disguise so that nobody would know who He was and there would be no lynching to contend with, and I said, yes, that wasn't a bad idea, but how would He disguise Himself and what would He look like and He asked if He could search my brain for an appropriate identity and become it for He still had that power.

I invited him to search to his heart's content and feel free to use anything He found there as His disguise, and as I sat under the tree, God darted into my earhole and I felt His divine light pierce my skull and wriggle around inside my brain.

"I don't know why he's searching your brain, when everything is inside mine," the philosopher grumbled.

After a few minutes of tingling around inside my brain God asked what was ole negar.

"Ole negar! No, God! Don't turn ole negar on me."

God said, Really, Baps, that is the perfect disguise—the image in your brain is very powerful. He would borrow the blueprint inside my brain and transform Himself into ole negar and that way we wouldn't have to put up with harassment, public

persecution and patriotic American family-value
lynching.

"No, God!" I bawled. "Not ole negar! Please, God!"

But before I could say another word, I heard a loud
whoosh, and right before my eyes the spark of light that
was God got fuzzy and clumped to form the figure of a
muscular black man who stood in front of me, grinning
like a nincompoop.

"Wha' happen, Baps?" He croaked. "You have any
white rum?"

"My word!" the philosopher gasped.

Chapter 15

The moment Almighty God became a regular ole negar it was worries from start to finish, what with the laziness, carousing, drinking binges, and endless vexations. When I would lose my temper and bark, "God! You going on too bad, you know!" He would belch, scratch his hairy belly, and beg me another lick of white rum.

During His incarnation as ole negar Almighty God proclaimed that His name was Egbert Adolphus Hackinton, and when I asked Him one morning as we sat talking in the tiny drawing room behind the shop why He'd chosen this particular name, He growled, "Lawd, Baps, don't ask me no fool-fool question, man!" Then He stood up and yawned without covering His mouth, exposing some gruesome cavities, and asked if I'd like to play some domino.

My mother always used to say, "If you can't say something good about somebody, don't say anything at all!" But she would also add, for she understood the value of a dirty secret, "But if you know something bad about somebody big, write down the particulars so you won't forget dem."

During God's incarnation as ole negar, I took her advice and carefully recorded His misdeeds in an exercise book, giving names, dates, times, offences, and places.

Much later, after God had changed back to His peenywally shape, I showed Him these notes and we both read them aloud and laughed, and He praised me for following my mother's sound advice.

"What is a modder for if not to give advice to a son?" I asked with humility. "And what son would be so ungrateful as not to heed de advice of a wise old modder?"

God shone His lovely light into my eyes and murmured, Baps, you are a saint.

"No, God!" I protested modestly. "I'm no saint. A saint would keep much neater notes dan dis!"

He glanced again at the rough scribbles and unpolished scratches I had haphazardly made in an exercise book and said, True, there had been a white man named Saint Augustine who used to raise Cain in Carthage before he gave up woman and who definitely kept neater notes.

"Well, God," I muttered, my feelings hurt at this implied criticism, "I did de best I could. And unlike dat white saint you mentioned, I never did give up woman. Let it be said dat I loved dem and grind dem faithfully through thick and thin to de bitter end."

God said, True, Nobody in his right mind could ever accuse me of that.

"Because I noticed dat when a Christian repent, de first thing him give up is woman! Even if woman have nothing at all to do with him criminality."

God said that it was plain to Him that I had never attended Catholic school.

We took an Air Jamaica jet to New York. We could have flown on our own, because all citizens of heaven can fly, but we wanted to travel in style and cock up our foot during the journey.

Plus we Jamaicans are a funny people. If we didn't fly on earth we just don't feel to fly in heaven. It's like a woman told me up there, she said, "Baps, I not flying. I'm no damn mosquito or John Crow. If you ever see me flying it mean only one thing: gunman push me off a precipice. When I travel, I take jet plane."

So we flew to New York by regular heavenly jet.

We landed in New York where we were processed by immigration officials and given visas for two months with the option of lengthening our stay into permanent status so long as we were willing to be dehooded and bleached white.

The man was polite and friendly but he was also firm and made us sign a paper agreeing to the conditions. He explained that visitors to America who retained their hoods were not allowed to exceed a two-month stay, for even a glimpse of earthly privates dangling from a crotch gave heavenly sheep trauma. Unbleached black visitors were also confined to a limited stay because black skin likewise gave sheep the heebie-jeebies.

While the man was checking us through immigration, the philosopher gaped around with amazement, puzzling no doubt about how all these many and varied wonders could fit inside his poor overcrowded brain.

We were inside a cavernous building that shimmered with a moonlit softness, and up near the rafters lolled some white men and women from a harp band who were on a break, squatting on a fleecy white cloud that hovered near the ceiling like an overhead bandstand. In the background wafted an annoying hallelujah like a whine of mosquitoes.

All the officials wore enormous wings complete with a full set of feathers, and all were dressed in billowing white robes that looked as if they had been spun from spiders' webs.

"Lawd God, what a way de music noisy!" Egbert complained, drawing a stern frown from the immigration official who reminded us that we were now in American heaven and should conduct ourselves in an appropriate way. He was in the middle of this scolding when a fat and fluffy sheep wandered into the cubicle and licked his knee with a friendly baa.

"Rass! Look 'pon dat sheep in de airport building!" Egbert bawled.

"This is my sheep, and I am his shepherd," the official said, rubbing behind the ears of the animal. "Say 'baaa' for the tourists," he urged the sheep, and the animal turned towards us and obediently baaed.

"Good heavens!" the philosopher muttered.

"Have a nice eternity," the official said, handing us our documents and turning back to the sheep that rubbed up against his leg beside a desk.

As we headed out of the terminal we heard him murmuring to the animal, "Did you safely graze today? Come, sit by my side. I will shelter thee from the wolf."

"Baps!" croaked Egbert, as we shuffled down the airport concourse. "I need a white rum bad!"

New York on earth is a sinkhole of human wastes, with towering buildings that make people feel like ants and air so dirty that it curdles in the crowded streets like a fart at a tea party.

But the New York of heaven has no skyscrapers, no cramped and smelly narrow streets with nasty asphalt tongues licking at the foundations of shiny glass buildings.

Centuries ago, I found out later, heaven's New York used to look just like earth's. Then because of Christian objections that the city wasn't properly Biblical, New York was razed and what we now stood gaping at built in its place.

Before us sprawled an oldtime Biblical city you might see in a child's bedtime tale, with a stone castle here and there squatting among single-storey red clay structures interlaced with unpaved streets on which a few white-robed pedestrians carrying shepherd's crooks quietly trudged. Fluttering above the streets was a steady flock of winged men and women dressed in fleecy white robes, carrying harps and crook sticks, their flapping wings making a breezy whoosh. The whole city—in fact, as I would find out later, all of heavenly America—looked fuzzy like beaten egg white.

We were gaping at the overhead river of flying people when all of a sudden the sky was filled with millions of wobbling wafers that came fluttering onto the streets like pin feathers.

"Baps!" Egbert bawled, covering his head with his hands. "Snow falling."

"It isn't snow, Pilgrim," chuckled an elderly robed gentleman who was walking past, "it's manna. It's lunch time."

Then he opened his mouth and stuck out his tongue as he sauntered away, gulping down the thickly falling flakes.

"Baps," Egbert wailed, "dis place weird! I want go back to Jamaica!"

The philosopher, meanwhile, was chomping on a mouthful of manna while the flakes piled up in thick drifts on the sidewalk.

"Hey! This is good!" he exclaimed.

We settled that first night in an inn off a quiet, tree-lined street. Naturally, we could have caroused all night, sleep in heaven being very sweet but not a necessity, except that after reaching new ground the first thing I always do is see how it sleeps. Plus, from what I could see, there was no place to carouse.

So I told Egbert that we should get an inn and catch a sleep, and he said he didn't mind so long as it was next to a rum bar or a dance hall. I explained to him that such things did not exist in American heaven, as far as I knew, and he grumbled, "So what de backside we doin' here?"

We slept well because everyone sleeps well in heaven, but all night long we heard a noisy bleating outside our window. The philosopher got up, opened the window and peered out into what looked like a backyard meadow teeming with a sea of fluffy sheep baying at the moon. Then he muttered that his brain was certainly funny and crawled back into bed.

"Baps," Egbert whispered in the darkness, "you don't hear dem sheep?"

"Yes," I said gruffly. "I hear dem."

"Baps, why you think dey have so much sheep in American heaven?"

"How would I know? Is you create dis place, not me."

"I never create nothing, Baps! What you talking 'bout?"

"Don't make no joke with me, you hear, God," I said. "Dis is serious. You know why dem have sheep up here."

"Baps," he said after a long moment filled up with sheeply baaing in the night, "you're a joker, you know dat?"

I lay in my bed and tried to think while the sheep bleated in the night and the philosopher snored.

Egbert shuffled out of bed, padded to the window, opened it and yelled into the darkness of the backyard meadow, "Shut up you rass mouth, sheep!"

"Hi, Egbert!" I protested. "Behave youself, man!"

A man dressed in shepherd's robes emerged out of the shadows and bawled up at the window, "Pilgrim, why dost thou bully my sheep?"

"Because dey baaing like bitch!" Egbert yelled back.

"Pilgrim," the man answered solemnly, "this is heaven. It is written that in heaven sheep shall graze and baa."

He muttered, "Written you rass," banged the window shut and flopped back into bed.

I groaned and said to myself, "Baps, you only just come to dis place called heaven, and look what you already do—mash up God and turn Him into ole negar. Dis is why you dead?"

Chapter 16

We went exploring the next morning, strolling through New York neighbourhoods.

Every house had a cloud floating above it like a kite, and as soon as the people walked out into the street and had their breakfast manna that rained down from the sky, they flew up to their private backyard cloud, sat down on it wearing white robes, and began harp-plunking.

Sometimes they flew up there carrying a sheep or two under their arms, and as we walked past we heard plunking and baaing drifting down from the same cloud. In some neighbourhoods the sheep would peer over the edge of the cloud as we walked past and baa at pedestrians. Egbert didn't like the cloud baaing and one time as a sheep baaed at him he turned around and bawled, "Hush you rass mouth, ole sheep!"

A robed shepherd stopped his harp-plunking and peered down at us over the edge of his cloud. "Foreigner," he cried, "wouldst thou like to sit on my cloud with me and my sheep?"

"Not a backside!" Egbert bawled. "I not sitting with no sheep 'pon no cloud! I am a Jamaican duppy! We don't walk wid sheep, we curry dem! We don't play fool-fool harp! We don't sit 'pon cloud!"

"You don't have to go one so bad, you know, man!" I hissed at him through the corner of my mouth. "Dis is dere country."

"I'll sit with you," cried the philosopher, floating up to the cloud, where we saw him peering over the edge beside the stranger while the sheep blasted a powerful nosehole baa right into his armpits.

"It's nice up here!" the philosopher yelled down to us.

"I going take a look," I said to Egbert.

He grabbed me by the arm. "Baps, is you bring me to dis madhouse! Now you goin' pitch on a backyard cloud and leave me alone inna de street?"

"Listen," I whispered, "you're God. Nobody can trouble you."

"My name is Egbert Adolphus Hackinton! I am a cultivator. Just because a man own a few acres o' land and a couple cow don't make him God, you know, Missah Socialist?"

It was no use arguing, ole negar personality had God so completely in its grip.

I flew up into the cloud and pitched beside the sheep.

Up there on the cloud, which was pink and stringy like cotton candy, there was fluffiness underfoot, and you could feel a gentle breeze. The sheep came over, sniffed at my crotch, gave a buck and bawled out a nasty baa.

"Foreigner, are you genitaled?" the cloud owner asked suspiciously.

"Of course. So, what you do with youself up here all day?"

The man looked nervous and uncomfortable. He flicked an edgy glance at the sheep that had backed up to a far corner of the cloud where it sat glaring at me and carrying on with a disgruntled baaing.

"Foreigner, you are frightening my sheep. He doth not abide shepherds who are genitaled."

"Tell him him safe. We weewee in chamber pot, not 'pon ole sheep."

The philosopher, meanwhile, had dropped flat on his back on the cloud and was wallowing in it like a hog in mud.

I walked over to the sheep and tried to pat the brute on the head but he gave a vicious buck and shied away, bouncing into the harp with his rump, causing it to tumble off the cloud and crash on the pavement next to where Egbert stood, peering up at us.

"Hey, you sheep!" Egbert bawled crossly. "You nearly bust me head wid you harp! You want me cook up you rass in a stewpot?"

We strolled up and down the city, and saw the same dreary sights everywhere we went.

We saw. no cars, no buses, no trucks, no taxis, no motorised transportation of any kind. Occasionally some dignitary would ride past on a donkey or a mule, and on Fifth Avenue we saw a bearded old gentleman sitting atop a camel plucking a portable harp as the beast swayed down the cobbled street.

We wandered into Central Park.

The park benches were gone, as was all the playground equipment and the tennis courts. But sheep abounded like weed.

Sheep was grazing on the walking trails, on the lawns, beside the lake, baaing up a storm. Where on earthly New York you were bound to find a mugger lurking in the bush to lick you down and thief you money, you found a sheep grazing with his shepherd strolling nearby, lugging a crook stick.

We shuffled out of the park and onto the street. Manna began falling in a thick rain of flakes.

"Kiss me neck!" Egbert grumbled. "It drizzling bread crumb again."

****

Around seven o'clock in the evening, we heard a tap on our door and the mistress of the house asked us if we'd like to attend a communal Last Supper. I stood hesitantly at the doorway and told her I didn't like the sound of that, but she said every night in households all over American heaven the Last Supper was celebrated as a daily custom. The philosopher, who was lying on his bed staring at the ceiling, ambled to the door and said we'd come, and the three of us joined other guests at the supper table.

We were served bread and grape juice the colour of red wine, and around the large banquet table the foreigners who were wearing ordinary clothes looked out of place with the native Americans, all of whom were Biblically robed.

An old gentleman from Turkey was sitting on my right. He said his bellybutton was almost fully grown, and he had travelled to the city to spend his last few weeks in heaven enjoying the brutality of New York's finest. He said that every day he'd been beaten up by the New York police, and on Wednesday he'd been pounded twice in the mornings and afternoons, and so far it was the most joyful vacation he'd ever had. Yesterday, in addition to having his head busted with a policeman's club, he'd been kicked down a gully by a patrolman's horse, and he thought he would die, the pain was so sweet.

Our landlord heaved a weary sigh at the head of the table.

"That is what's wrong with this country!" he said in an exasperated voice. "There's no real pain. There's no discomfort. Everything is immoral pleasure. And it's all God's fault!"

"No, it's not," contradicted the philosopher with a boasty smirk, nibbling on a crust of bread. "It's my fault."

"Hush up you mouth," I hissed at him.

"When I found out that there was no hell," a young mother said with a quaver in her voice and a tremble to her lip, "I thought I would die."

"There, there, Alice!" her husband comforted her.

"I realised that all I'd worked for on earth, all the good I'd tried so hard to do all my life, meant nothing. Everyone is ruthlessly happy here, even vicious, drunken Mr. Leonard from the old neighbourhood in Iowa who used to beat his wife."

"Mom!" their little boy cried at her distress, cuddling up to console her.

"All the Girl Scout cookies I sold! The blood drives I organised! The Meals-on-Wheels I delivered to the homebound! The no-sex on Sunday rule I put my poor husband through."

The husband sighed over woeful earthly memory.

"For what? To share heaven with nasty Mr. Leonard, who beat his wife, who was always drunk, who never did an honest day's work in all his life, and who probably had sex twice on Sundays? And you know what's even more infuriating? I'm happy! Right now, even as I cry about my wasted, unappreciated Christian life on earth, I'm happy! I'm deliriously happy."

Here she burst into an uncontrollable sobbing broken by maniacal bursts of laughter. Her husband struggled to comfort her, as did her child, and all three of them soon dissolved in a show of family merriment through the streaming tears.

"Never mind, ma'am," our landlord said philosophically. "One day our scientists will figure out how to capture God. We'll make Him pay. And we'll make Him change things, too!"

"You leave God alone!" I snapped.

"Oh, you're one of those foreign God-lovers, eh?" the landlord said sarcastically.

"God is my friend!" I growled indignantly.

"I wouldn't say that too loud over here, if I were you," one of the diners at the end of the table muttered darkly.

A tremor of grumbling rolled around the table, especially among the clotted groups of robed Americans. Several diners glared at me. On earth, they would have definitely charged and lynched me from a lamppost. But up here, the dogs-in-the-manger spitefully decided to withhold the pleasure of the rope.

The uncomfortable silence was broken by our landlord.

"We Americans are an enterprising people!" he boasted patriotically. "Our scientists are working on a vaccine to instil real pain even as we speak. We'll have pain up here, sooner or later. We'll have our hell. Its fire will sear flesh, singe hair, and really hurt. Sinners will shriek. Fornicators will howl. Adulterers will tremble and shake. Just wait!"

"Do you know," remarked the philosopher, turning to the old gentleman from Turkey, "the most amazing thing, now that you mention it. I have a fully-grown bellybutton, too."

He peeled open his shirt and exposed a knobby bellybutton as thick and swollen as Miss B's had been.

"Oh," exclaimed the old Turkish gentleman, "that's a big one. Want to come out with me tomorrow? I can promise you a good beating. You might even get kicked in the head by the police horse."

The philosopher shook his head and muttered that there was no sheep, no policeman, and certainly no pleasurable beating.

I asked the Turkish gentleman what he did to provoke the beating and kicking and he chuckled and said he unzipped his fly and flashed the sheep.

"Exposing yourself to peaceful Christian American sheep?" the mother challenged nastily. "That's a wholesome hobby?"

"It's a pastime," the old gentleman shrugged, adding modestly, "I don't have much time left up here. I think the sheep like it. Especially the ewes."

"Our sheep do not like it!" the woman shrieked, red-faced and glaring. Then, she added with a high-pitched laugh, "And hearing your sick story makes me very happy, too! I hate this heaven! I want to go back to Iowa!"

"No pain," our landlord sighed. "How can you have heaven without pain? It's impossible!"

Egbert leaned over and whispered, "Baps! What a weird set of people, eh?"

Chapter 17

Everywhere we travelled in New York we heard the same complaints from Americans: they couldn't stand that there was no pain in heaven; that they always felt happy even though they had the Constitutional right to feel miserable; that a crook got the same size backyard cloud as a baptised Christian; that a murderer executed on earthly Texas could brazenly walk the streets of heaven among decent citizens like the wretch had belonged to the Dallas Chamber of Commerce.

I met a gentleman from Chicago and he explained to me that without a hell, there was no point in heaven. He told me that on earth he had been a loyal Republican, a taxpayer, a war veteran, and if he had known he would die and go to Democrat heaven, he would have killed himself. I asked him what difference killing himself would have made, and he said that suicides went immediately back to earth, taking the shape of the first available body—whether human, worm, animal, or bug. He was quite bitter and said that even if he had recycled back to earth as a dog and ended up in a Chinyman's stew pot it would still have been better than to find himself in a nasty Democrat heaven where thrifty wage-earners had to enjoy the same pleasures as hardened gas guzzlers and crooks.

I asked him why he kept calling it a democrat heaven and he growled and said because it was just like the kind of heaven a pork-barrel Democrat hog would think up: freeness everywhere; compulsory laughter and joy; no struggle or pain. He said that in Republican heaven every man would have a different size cloud depending on his own initiative and sweat. None of this ugly standardisation of cloud, sheep and harp. If a soul worked hard, he would earn a bigger cloud, louder harp, fatter sheep. If he was idle and good-for-nothing, he would end up on a mash-up cloud with only one scrawny sheep for company. And if he didn't make his monthly payments the bank would repossess his cloud and pitch him out on the street.

"You can't have homeless man in heaven!" I objected.

"Why not?" he growled.

"Because de man is dead. Him reach heaven!"

"That's just a technicality," he snapped. Then he added, "Maybe God isn't moral, but America is!"

And even as he was grumbling about this, he was laughing for he was happy—poor chap.

One morning we came out of our lodgings and found crowds milling about on the sidewalks. We asked a passing stranger what was happening and he told us that today was "Hell Day," and that everyone was waiting for the grand parade to start.

At first I thought he was running a joke, but as we mixed up with the throng, we kept hearing excited chatter about national "Hell Day," about how it was even better than Thanksgiving, and realised that we were witnessing the festivities of an American federal holiday. Berobed citizens and their flocks of sheep milled about on the sidewalks, wearing an air of revelry and excitement.

We jostled our way into the crowds and gawked as floats sponsored by various civic organisations and drawn by harnessed sheep lumbered past, depicting scenes from an imaginary hell.

For example, I remember that one float rumbling past showed a fiery dungeon of torture in which horned demons chopped off the heads of sinners over and over again, causing the volunteers playing the parts of the damned to squeal with delight at each whack of the axe and ruin an otherwise horrible spectacle. The float rattled down the cobbled street drawn by about forty sheep draped with signs notifying the public that it had been constructed by the Kiwanis Club of Brooklyn at its own expense and donated in the spirit of good citizenship. Applause rippled through the crowd as the axe cut off the sinner's head, causing it to bounce on the floor of the float like a beach ball, until it snapped back onto the bloody neck stump.

Another float, put on by an association of American women, featured a damned male fornicator hanging upside down from a wooden pole and being lowered into a boiling pot of bubbling oil by stern demonettes. One demonette had clamped the volunteer's imagined privates (he had none, for he had been governmentally dehooded) with a pair of red-hot pliers and was pretending to crack his earthly balls. Naturally, the young man playing the part of the upside down fornicator was quite jolly, and every time he was dunked into the scalding oil, his peals of laughter rolled over the parade route, causing some disgruntlement among the crowds of onlookers who understood, however, that the poor fellow could not help expressing compulsory bliss.

Float after float showed similar scenes of wicked torture and cruelty that the sponsoring civic group thought belonged in hell. The parade of rumbling hell floats brought out my indoor parson from where he had been skulking, causing him to occasionally bawl, "Yes, sah! Now you talking!" much to the delight of nearby spectators, some of whom clapped me jovially on the back and congratulated me on having good sense for a foreigner.

As the parade clattered slowly past, the only incident to mar the festivities was the uncouth behaviour of rude-boy youths who charged the floats and demanded that the costumed demons torment them, too, or they would stone the parade. The demon volunteers, for the sake of peace, would dutifully lash out at the rudies prancing beside the rumbling floats, slashing them with butcher knives or pouring molten lead over their bodies, causing them to dance and squeal with sheer joy, spoiling the solemnity of the occasion.

"Juvenile delinquents!" I heard an elderly gentleman grumble.

"What an ugly generation," a well-dressed American lady sighed.

The crowd occasionally booed these spirited youngsters, and once in a while an indignant member of the clergy or bearded civic leader would charge among them and add to their merriment with a few good thumps.

Egbert, meanwhile, through all the confusion and noise, had curled up against the wall of a building and fallen asleep, snoring so loudly that he attracted glowering stares of disapproval from some in the crowd. One man standing next to me suggested to the others that they lynch the impious foreigner, and another hurried off, saying he was going to get a rope.

I elbowed my way through the crowd and warned Egbert to wake up, or he would presently be lynched. He stirred and peered up drowsily at me just as the Grand Prize-winning float rumbled past, showing a mechanical worm gnawing its way into a sinner's wide-open eyeball, its tail wriggling in the air and batting against eyelash, while the sinner shrieked and laughed from all the fun. On a platform in the rear of that particular float perched four harpists who played a hymn about "Gnawing Out Eyeball of Sinner On The Appointed Day," drawing rounds of good-hearted, patriotic applause from the keenly watching citizens.

"A worm eating out a sinner's eyeball! Is this a great country or what?" a matronly American lady squatting on the pavement beside Egbert chortled, her chest bursting with national pride.

"Egbert!" I nudged God, leaning over to whisper. "Wake up! Dem gone to get a rope to come lynch you."

He rubbed his eyes sleepily. "What me do?"

"You snore on dem parade. You hurt dem patriotic feelings. Come! Make we go before dem come back wid de rope."

He stood up unsteadily and peered around at the endless sea of bobbing heads gawking at the passing floats. I could see the gang of glaring patriots still scowling at us. The philosopher ambled over and sniffed.

"I don't quite know what to make of this," he confessed, looking bedraggled with confusion. "I was never a religious man."

"Shut up and help me with Egbert," I hissed. "Patriots coming to lynch him."

"Baps," Egbert mumbled, weaving like he was drunk from too much rum or spectacle, "dis is a funny people. I want go home to Jamaica."

The patriots saw that we were slinking off, and one of them shoved his way angrily over to detain us. I gave him a quick kick in his crotch, feeling nothing but an empty spot where hood and balls had once roosted on earth, and he doubled over and gasped, "Ohhh! That was good! Do it again!"

I did as he asked, this time dropping him flat on the sidewalk, where he sprawled against the thick cluster of legs, while we wormed our way through the "ohhing" and "aahing" of onlookers.

As I shoved Egbert ahead of me I caught a whiff of white rum on his breath.

"You been drinking rum!"

He mumbled that he'd found a bottle of white rum on the pavement and had had a tups.

"Will you kick me again, please!" the patriot begged, catching up to us and grabbing at my shirt.

"No! Brute!" I snapped in his face. "You was going lynch me friend. Go home!"

I had my hands full with Egbert, trying to push him through the crowd, but the patriot continued to chase after us, begging a kick. Finally, I snarled at the philosopher, "Make youself useful and kick de wretch for me, nuh?"

He said that he'd try his best, and as we eased away I heard a wishy-washy thud followed by an indignant squeal, "You call that a kick?"

Then we were out of earshot and darting across the street between the clattering floats.

I had to laugh. "You know," I told Egbert, "I can see why dese people vex with you. Taking away pain and suffering ruin dere American way of life."

"Baps! Make me go drink a rum."

The crowd exploded into a jubilant cheer and I turned in time to see the Lion's Club float rumbling past, showing a man wearing a sign that said "murderer" around his neck. He lay on his back, his naked belly torn open, while a flock of mechanical vultures buried their

---

beaks in his exposed liver, making him laugh like they were pecking his funny bone.

"I don't understand why you kick so much better than I do when everything is inside my head," the philosopher grumbled, worming his way through the crush of onlookers to stand beside us. "How did that happen?"

Chapter 18

We travelled to Chicago and then to Detroit. Everywhere we went we encountered sheep, backyard cloud, rampant harp playing, and daily manna drizzle.

We drifted north to Maine, where me and the philosopher had it out one night as we were camping out in a woodland.

It began when I said that the Maine sheep baaed through their nose, while the New York sheep had a throaty baa like gargling, and the philosopher said that it was the same baa and he should know for all baaing took place inside his head.

Egbert, meanwhile, had propped himself up against the trunk of a pine tree where he was drinking rum and gazing around the campsite like a boy scout leader looking to molest a tenderfoot.

"Listen," I said to the philosopher, losing my temper, "is time you realise dat all baaing not in you head! Not even a single, solitary sheep in you head. Face facts. You dead. You in heaven. I not in you head. Heavenly ram and ewe and lamb not in you head. And that man over there drinking rum is God in disguise. And God is definitely not....."

I stopped suddenly in mid-sentence for I had heard a twig snap.

I scanned the ragged fringe of dark woods dancing to the flames of our campfire. "Who dat?"

The philosopher looked up. "What's the matter?"

"Somebody out dere! You don't hear dat sound?"

He said he'd heard nothing, but I jumped up and charged a trembling bush.

I hauled a shepherd I found crouching there into the glow of the fire. Two small sheep trotted after him meekly.

"Why you hiding behind dat bush?" I demanded, draping him up like a constable.

"I'm not hiding," he squirmed. "I was grazing my sheep in the starlight."

"Don't tell me no lie, or I'll thump you down."

"Oh, would you please?"

I noticed that he was boring into Egbert with his eyeball, so I shook the brute and asked him what he was looking at. He mumbled nothing, and begged me to please deliver the promised thump and let him go.

I released him and ordered him out of our camp. As he left, he turned to give Egbert another lingering stare.

With the shepherd gone, we tried to settle down for the night.

The stars were blazing overhead in a clear sky, and there was a nail-clipped moon fastened to the horizon like a hookworm.

I was just beginning to doze off when the philosopher mumbled, "I don't feel too steady. My head feels woozy. Does it look funny?"

In the light of the campfire, which was chewing on scraps of darkness, I glanced up and immediately saw that he was crowning, that his headtop was disappearing.

"Backside, man!" I gasped, jumping to my feet. "You getting born again!"

"Rubbish," he said airily. "Once you're dead, you're dead."

"Feel you headtop! Half of it gone already!"

He groped for his head with his hand, and by then his whole face had been clean shaved off and only a stumpy neck remained that was dropping fast.

"Must be another hallucination," he mumbled.

"You getting born again, man! Look! Only a small chunk o' neckbone left!"

"Don't get so excited. There's a logical explanation."

"Rass! Now all shoulder gone!"

He shifted against the tree as if making himself comfortable for the night.

"I know none of this is happening," he said, in the hollow voice Miss B had used once her own head had disappeared. "This shouldn't be. Therefore it isn't."

I felt like kicking the wretch, but there was hardly anything left to kick, for his waist had melted down and only two thick unattached legs remained that wriggled and squirmed over the grass.

Evenly, smoothly, as if his flesh and bone were being silently siphoned off, the philosopher melted down to ankle bone.

"Goodbye, Mr. Philosopher!" I bawled. "Maybe I'll see you one day down on earth."

"I'm not going anywhere," he echoed stubbornly.

Another twitch of his stubby, footless toes, and he was gone.

In the dimness I felt for any trace of him. Nothing remained behind but a slight warm dip in the grass where his body had just rested.

"God, look," I cried, "the philosopher born again."

"Baps, stop calling me God," Egbert growled crossly. "It's very provoking."

Chapter 19

I must have dozed off for a few hours. When I awoke it was still dark, and God had changed back to His peenywally shape and was flitting about my head like a sliver of summer sun.

"God!" I cried, jumping up. "Why you change back? Mind American patriot see you, you know!"

God said that He felt to eat a star.

I stood up and stretched sleepy neckstring and backbone and asked Him to repeat what He'd said, and He said He wouldn't be long, He just thought He'd browse in the Orion constellation and gobble down a nova or two. He asked if I'd like to come along or would I like to sleep while He did what He needed to do.

I didn't understand, but I said I'd come along anyway.

Touch my light, Baps, God commanded.

I reached out and touched the ring of brightness that sparkled from His peenywally body.

We blew into the dark heavens like a blast from a twelve-bore shotgun.

We were past the moon before my first blink, and even before my second blink, we had zoomed clear of the flabby yellow rind of the sun.

Swiftly, silently, breezelessly, surrounded by a trillion granulated grains of stars, we soared through the bottomless ocean of darkness, which felt so sweet and cool that I told God I was going to take off my clothes and skinny dip in the milky glow if He didn't mind.

God laughed and said, Do what you want, so I shed my clothes and watched them tumble away in cool, raw space while my parson bawled, "Flying naked through heaven! Exposing de purity of starlight to nasty batty hole! What you going do next, grind de universe?"

Pearly starlight brushed my nakedness like cool spring water, and I gloried in the exaltation of winging through the heavens on the shimmering light of God.

We rocketed into a brilliant cluster of stars, and Almighty God dove right into the burning furnace of the brightest nova and began to eat it out like a sugar bun.

Before my eyes, even as I stared, the fiery nova shrivelled up as God sucked out the juice of its starlight, turning it into a wobbly black clot.

"God!" I bawled. "You eat up de star!"

God sparked out of the dark heart of the eaten-up star, blazing with a brightness that dazzled my eyes.

A chunk of jagged rockstone slowly rolled out of the darkness. I grabbed onto it and tumbled through cool space as God ate another star, sucking out its sparkle and leaving a black pit.

God was now so bright that human eye couldn't behold Him without burning up, but since I was a duppy I could steal a glance every now and again, but even duppy eye had to watch out for the brightness.

God said He was done and told me to touch His light. On the way back down, I collected my clothes and dressed in the cool fluorescence of starlight.

We zoomed through space and landed on the moon.

There we had a heartfelt man-to-God chat.

You should have seen me, Taddeus Baps, cock up my foot on a cracked rim of the moon while me and God exchanged thoughts about this and that.

From the socket of black space, the blue earth peered at us like an unwinking German eyeball.

I told God about the philosopher and God said that this was the third time he had died and been reborn without knowing it.

"Dis is deep, God," I muttered. "Dead and reach heaven three times and don't even know it. What a waste of life!"

God replied that the philosopher was a *shouldist* and that *shouldists* were stubborn people.

"*Shouldist*? What you call a *shouldist*?"

God said that a *shouldist* was one who insists on remaking the world as he thinks it *should* be, rather than accepting it as it is.

He said the philosopher thought that there should be no life after death, and when he found out that there was, rather than change his opinion, he clung stubbornly to his *should*.

God was in a deep mood—right away I could see that.

But I have my deep side, too, even though I usually hide it from ole negar, and God and the moon were drawing depth out of me.

"Look, God," I said. "Most teacher would tell you that the rule of *should* is good—that *should* make you brush you hair in the morning, you teeth at night, take Sunday bath, rinse you frock and iron up you good pants, don't cuss bad word, and behave youself in public. Better a *shouldist* than a hooligan."

God said, Point, Baps. A little *should* is fine. But a lot of *should* leads to principle and principle leads to murder.

I had to chuckle. "God," I advised, "draw brake awhile. How principle lead to murder?"

God said, Consider this Baps, you meet your neighbour on the street one morning, what do you think the neighbour should do?

"Say 'good morning'. That is just good manners."

And suppose your neighbour doesn't say 'good morning', what do you do?

"I might tell him 'bout his backside or lick him down."

Why don't you say 'good morning'?

"God," I tried to be as calm as possible, for it was obvious that God didn't understand dealings with ill-bred neighbour, "is de principle. If my neighbour come and see me on de street, he should say 'good morning' first."

But suppose, Baps, your neighbour thinks the same about you—that you should bid him 'good morning' first?

"Is not dat simple, you know, God. A man must stand for some principle. And it is my neighbour's bounden duty to say 'good morning' if he comes and sees me on the street."

See, Baps. That's the poison of *shouldism*.

I didn't want to argue with God on the moon, so I changed the subject and asked God how come He had eaten the stars, if He was hungry or if He just felt like nibbling up some of His universe for a joke, and He explained His everlasting mystery to me, Taddeus Baps.

He said that He needed to eat a star every now and again, that earthly scientists called the eaten-out star scrap a Black Hole, and that if you searched the universe long and hard enough you could tell where He'd had His Last Supper.

He said that everything I beheld around me, the billion rhinestone specks of stars, the rimless darkness of space, the crumbly circumference of the moon, used to be a part of Him.

He explained that He had used Himself as raw material to create the universe. That was why He had become so tiny and powerless—because everything of Himself had gone into His handiwork of creation.

"So every now and again you need to eat part of it back?"

Exactly, God said, especially when He was put under strain or pressure.

"Being ole negar put You under a strain, eh?"

God said, Whew! Baps! That was a celestial pressure!

"Of course is celestial pressure. You think ole negar easy? You shoulda never create dem!"

God said, He didn't, that I did.

"Hear dis now!" I blared sarcastically. "Poor Baps create all de million of ole negar dat mash up de world! Is Baps tell you to get drunk and carouse and carry on like a hooligan when you was Egbert? Is Baps make you go on so bad?"

God said He had behaved in the image and likeness of ole negar that dwelled within my mind. He had been as I thought ole negar *should* be.

Even my indoor parson jumped to my defence.

He sneered, "Dis stupid, sinful shopkeeper couldn't even build a chicken coop much create less one ole negar."

A man is not just flesh and bone, Baps. A man is also an idea. And the idea behind a man is what makes him what he is, good or evil.

"So you saying dere's good in ole negar?"

Yes, Baps, there's good in the heart of all who walk the world.

"Boy," I muttered gloomily, "it look like neighbour and ole negar just not Your strong suit, God."

God said He could easily prove His point if I agreed to a simple experiment.

"What experiment?"

He said that He'd like to change me into Egbert so I could dwell inside the flesh and bone of my own creation.

"What? Me? Become ole negar?"

Yes.

"I, Taddeus Baps, who graduate from de University of de West Indies, former tutor at Excelsior College, must now, at dis advanced stage in my life, dead and reach heaven to turn into ole negar?"

Unless, of course, God said quietly, you're afraid.

"Listen, God! Don't make me raise me voice and go on bad on de moon! But learn dis, BAPS NOT 'FRAID OF NO OLE NEGAR!"

So you'll become one?

"I'll become a hundred ole negar if You like, to prove de point! I never create dem! I don't make dem go on bad! I don't foster dere indiscipline and wayward nature! I don't make dem worship de idols of rum, dancehall and canepiece pumpum! Dese are Your creations, not mine! And all You going accomplish when You turn me into ole negar, is make me shame me Mummy!"

I must admit that I was indignant and vexed as I cocked up my foot on the crust of the moon and mashed brains with God.

But when we came back down to the Maine campfire beside the woodland, God had assumed my shape and I had become Egbert Adolphus Hackinton, one of the worst ole negar to ever walk the face of the earth.

Chapter 20

Notice to the Reading Public: This chapter has been edited by barrister.

Barristeristic editing was necessary to protect myself from criminal proceedings. I have asked barrister to read this chapter and cross out whatever material might blacken my good name and would make me liable to lawsuit. Any objectionable material, at barrister's discretion, is crossed out so:

***********Crossed out by Barrister**********

Over the next few days while I was Edgar Adolphus, I experienced serious worries. I craved praedial larceny. I thirsted for demon rum. I lusted after pumpum. I longed to capture idle land. My mentality hungered for socialism, grant-in-aid, scholarship money, and government freeness. I yearned to stone a neighbour's mango tree. My brain was crammed full of speculations and thoughts about subjects I knew nothing about.

I went on bad in various ways. I admit it now that I look back. I don't want to get into all the nasty details of my uncouth behaviour. Suffice it is to say that I was not myself, and barrister assures me that because I had been converted into ole negar through an Act of God, I cannot be held legally liable.

One time, for instance, as we were flying over Wyoming, I spotted a plump shepherd girl tending her flock of sheep on the prairie and, bawling to God that I would soon come, I flew down to put rude arguments to her.

At first she was pleasant and we had a nice conversation about this and that as I softened her up with speechification on popular topics.

She said that she lived on a nearby farm, and that she was tending her father's flock while he spent the day tuning his harp for a concert that Sunday in church.

I boasted that no harp was ever made that my hand couldn't tune, and she said that perhaps I would like to fly over to her father's farm with her and help with the harp-tuning, and I replied, certainly, but before we went why didn't we sit in the shade of a tree away from the grazing sheep and discuss the why's and wherefore's of offshore banking.

She agreed and we sat down in the shade a leafy tree.

What happened next is fuzzy. But I do remember her chucking me off, boxing my ears, and bawling, "Foreign sinner! I am decently caulked!"

"Caulked!" I heard myself scoffing. "Anything American government can caulk, I can uncaulk," and as I said this I*********Crossed out by Barrister*********

As we lay panting after our scuffle, I asked her gruffly, "You sheep caulk, too?"

"My innocent sheep?" she shrieked.

"Who say dem innocent? Dem sheep come like church sister—dem just pretend. Like say, look 'pon dat nice fat ewe over dere ***********Crossed out by Barrister*********

Later, I rejoined God and flew glumly over the lush prairieland where for miles and miles you saw nothing but ripples in the grass and the occasional pasture cloud on which a country-boy angel pitched with his harp and rural sheep.

"Dey caulk everything female on dis whole continent. What is wrong with dese people," I heard myself muttering to God.

Shouldism, God replied.

Looking back on this adventure, I realise now that I very nearly became a sheep grinder during our prairie adventure. Many months afterwards, when I had once again been transformed into Baps, I complained bitterly to God about the risk he'd made me run by turning me into ole negar in paradise.

"You hear de argument I put to de woman about her ewe," I griped. "Is a lucky thing I never end up grinding some nasty prairie Wyoming sheep! Is dat why I work so hard on earth to build up me three shops? So I could dead and end up in heaven as a nasty sheep grinder?"

Baps, God said humorously, that would never have happened.

"Why? You stay dere thinking ole negar can't grind sheep. You want see what dem do to Jamaican goat. Why you think country people nowadays 'fraid to drink goat milk?"

Baps, I tell you, that would never have happened.

"Why not? Because of fool-fool caulking? Nothing American government can caulk dat Jamaica ole negar can't uncaulk!"

Baps, you worry too much, God said.

Among the other degenerate acts I attempted to perform during this most trying period of my life were
**********Crossed out by Barrister*********
**********Crossed out by Barrister*********
**********Crossed out by Barrister*********
**********Crossed out by Barrister*********

***********Crossed out by Barrister*********
***********Crossed out by Barrister*********
***********Crossed out by Barrister*********
***********Crossed out by Barrister*********
***********Crossed out by Barrister*********
***********Crossed out by Barrister*********
***********Crossed out by Barrister*********
***********Crossed out by Barrister*********
***********Crossed out by Barrister*********
***********Crossed out by Barrister*********
***********Crossed out by Barrister*********
***********Crossed out by Barrister*********
***********Crossed out by Barrister*********
***********Crossed out by Barrister*********
***********Crossed out by Barrister*********
***********Crossed out by Barrister*********
***********Crossed out by Barrister*********
***********Crossed out by Barrister*********
***********Crossed out by Barrister*********
***********Crossed out by Barrister*********
***********Crossed out by Barrister*********
***********Crossed out by Barrister*********
***********Crossed out by Barrister*********
***********Crossed out by Barrister*********
***********Crossed out by Barrister*********
***********Crossed out by Barrister*********
***********Crossed out by Barrister*********
***********Crossed out by Barrister*********
***********Crossed out by Barrister*********
***********Crossed out by Barrister*********
***********Crossed out by Barrister*********
***********Crossed out by Barrister*********
***********Crossed out by Barrister*********

***********Crossed out by Barrister**********
***********Crossed out by Barrister**********
***********Crossed out by Barrister**********
***********Crossed out by Barrister**********
***********Crossed out by Barrister**********
***********Crossed out by Barrister**********
***********Crossed out by Barrister**********
***********Crossed out by Barrister**********
***********Crossed out by Barrister**********
***********Crossed out by Barrister**********
***********Crossed out by Barrister**********
***********Crossed out by Barrister**********
***********Crossed out by Barrister**********
***********Crossed out by Barrister**********
***********Crossed out by Barrister**********
***********Crossed out by Barrister**********
***********Crossed out by Barrister**********
***********Crossed out by Barrister**********
***********Crossed out by Barrister**********
***********Crossed out by Barrister**********
***********Crossed out by Barrister**********
***********Crossed out by Barrister**********
***********Crossed out by Barrister**********
***********Crossed out by Barrister**********
***********Crossed out by Barrister**********
***********Crossed out by Barrister**********
***********Crossed out by Barrister**********
***********Crossed out by Barrister**********
***********Crossed out by Barrister**********
***********Crossed out by Barrister**********
***********Crossed out by Barrister**********
***********Crossed out by Barrister**********
***********Crossed out by Barrister**********
***********Crossed out by Barrister**********

***********Crossed out by Barrister**********
***********Crossed out by Barrister**********
***********Crossed out by Barrister**********
***********Crossed out by Barrister**********
***********Crossed out by Barrister**********
***********Crossed out by Barrister**********
***********Crossed out by Barrister**********
***********Crossed out by Barrister**********
***********Crossed out by Barrister**********
***********Crossed out by Barrister**********
***********Crossed out by Barrister**********
***********Crossed out by Barrister**********

On advice from barrister, this chapter is hereby terminated.

Chapter 21

Given the chance, would Jamaican ole negar—out of the goodness of his heart—risk life and limb to rescue God from capture, experimentation, probe, and assault?

The answer, from the Chapter to follow, is *yes*.

Now before the reader laughs scornfully in my face and flings this book across the room or uses its leaves to wipe batty, please be assured that it is not I, Taddeus Baps, who clings to this wayward opinion. It is Almighty God.

I have tried to convince God that to so wilfully interpret the events I am about to relate and insist that a ole negar named Egbert Adolphus Hackington tried to rescue Him could make Him a laughingstock among Jamaica's congregations and bring back the public worship of Baal.

I have also tried to point out to Him that it is an act of colonialism to venture onto our shores and try to gainsay what we Jamaicans know to be unshakeable truths about the most degenerate members of our population.

Of course, God, having created everything, thinks He's entitled.

Squeamish readers are strongly advised to skip this chapter.

I was still Egbert Adolphus Hackington—a hardened Jamaican ole negar. I was not Baps.

On my brain I bore the heavy burden of ole negar thoughts and appetites—foremost among them being rum and pumpum, followed by praedial larceny, petty theft, and hopes for a prosperous cock-up-foot-on-veranda retirement after bank embezzlement.

I had been guzzling rum hard that day and had tried my best to get a backslider ewe drunk—for what nasty purpose I cannot even begin to guess. God was putting up with my antics and listening with amusement to my stupid opinions as we flew over the rippling prairie grass in a breeze. Occasionally, I'd swoop down to the ground and try to speechify some shepherd girl I'd spotted roaming the grasslands with her flock only to learn that she, too, had been patriotically caulked. Then I'd rejoin God and try to explain to him what caused biliousness in Kingstonians, why Chinyman was no good at domino, or why crab louse love to prowl in a full moon, all of which God seemed eager to learn.

Eventually, since it was getting dark, me and God landed on a desolate stretch of prairie and built a campfire. We sat around chatting for an hour or so, or at least I was chatting and God was listening, then I had a snort of white rum and went to sleep.

That night, after sleeping for an hour or so, I woke on the prairie and found myself surrounded by a gang of gunmen leaning down over me and shining bright lights in my face, chattering like street vendors who had backed up a tourist.

"Hey!" I bawled, jumping up.

Out of the blur one of them shot a gun at me. It made a whooshing sound and sprayed a watery light that coiled over my head and around my body like a gummy spider web.

"You got him!" a soldier yelled. "Blast him again with the God ray if he gives trouble."

I peered at the dim shapes around me in the glare of the lights and recognised among them the shepherd we had met in the field a few days earlier.

"That's God in disguise!" he bawled.

A burly man in uniform stepped out of the lights and laid a rough hand on my shoulder. He was dressed in a military uniform with a ramgoat embroidered on his khaki shirt.

"In the name of the American government, I place you, God, under arrest," he said gruffly.

Now as every logical reader knows, a regular Jamaican ole negar would have bawled, "Who you calling God?" and boxed down the soldier before running off like a thief.

But all the wholesale caulking of female species in Wyoming must have put me under such pressure that I cracked.

This much I immediately knew: the so-called God ray that they had shot at me was rubbish. I could easily break out of it anytime and thump down the whole bitch lot of them.

I almost did, too, except that I thought, at that instant, that God, who was most likely flying somewhere around the place, was not as rough and tough as me and might not be able to withstand the shot.

I decided then and there to pretend to be helpless before their bogus God-gun to give God the chance to escape back to Jamaica.

And I supposedly did this good deed while I was ole negar incarnate, while I was not myself but Egbert Theophilus Hackington. My actions, says God, proved the truth of His words when He said unto me, *Yea, Baps, there's good in the heart of all who walk the world. Even ole negar.*

The next page is for public thumping. It is left purposefully blank as a convenience to suffering readers who, outraged at this cock-and-bull story about ole negar's supposed goodheartedness, now strongly desire to thump down this book.

Thump This Page

The troops bundled me into a truck, and our small convoy rumbled across the prairie. There was no road and the ride over the dark grassland was rough and bumpy.

I was sandwiched in between two soldiers, one of whom, a hefty young man on my right, whispered to me that he was sorry for helping capture me, but he was only doing his job.

"Doing thy job!" I scorned. "Dost thou not know that I can change thy testicles into naseberry with one flick of my finger?"

"The government took my testicles," he muttered crossly.

"Fool with thy God, and I will re-plant testicles on thy worthless crotch!"

"Listen, God!" he whispered furtively out of his mouth corner. "Why be so hard-headed? Nobody wants to hurt You. We know You created us. And we appreciate it. Just last night I said to my wife, 'You know, I wouldn't even mind if God joined our softball team'."

"God plays cricket, idiot!"

"Well, if You played softball, I'd let You join our team. That's because I appreciate You. But You've got to understand, this universe is not up to American standards. It's got to change."

"One more word, and I smite," I growled.

"I've had my shots. Not even God can smite a patriotic American who's had his shots."

We rumbled over the dark prairie the rest of the way in a grim silence.

Our journey ended at midmorning when the convoy pulled into an underground depot, and I was escorted

Where was God? Why had he left me looking like Egbert Adolphus Hackington?

I tried to remember what had happened. Most likely God was off gourmandizing stars while abandoning me on the prairie to be gunned down by the American ramgoat army. Probably He hadn't even noticed that while He was gobbling down stars, I was getting my backside blasted with rays meant for Him. But I notice that's how the world goes: while the head man is out enjoying life, carousing and gallivanting with the conniving secretary, the little, hardworking clerk is busy absorbing corporate gunshot wound.

I was trying to decide what to do next when I heard feet tramping down the corridor and a detachment of guards carrying loaded ray guns came and marched me down to a laboratory.

They escorted me, side by side, into a room that looked like it belonged in a Frankenstein movie. Scientific equipment was humming all over the place, with lights flashing and screens blipping, and they put me through tests galore ranging from poking me with finger to touching me with electronic probe to aiming instruments at my eyeball and shooting rays at my person.

I put up with it all. I gave no argument and back-talked no technician, except when they took me into a small cubicle.

"You have to take off your pants for this probe," a technician said gruffly.

"Which part you goin' probe?"

"You'll see."

"Not a rass. No probe. No trousers coming off."

The guard levelled his ray gun at me.

"Take off your pants off," snapped the technician, "or he'll shoot."

"In heaven or on earth, only woman is authorised to pull down my trousers."

"Shoot him until he obeys," the technician ordered the guard.

The guard blasted me at point-blank range with the ray gun. I jumped off the table, pushed aside the curtain of the cubicle, ripped the gun from his hands and flung it across the room.

"Hey!" he yelled, blowing a whistle.

Guards swarmed into the room and tried to drape me up and hold me down, but I thumped right and left, floored three with one right hand and two with one left, and made my way down the corridor with about six of them hanging onto me and trying to prevent my escape.

Of course, it was no use. In heaven you can't force anyone to do what he doesn't want to do, and no matter if you bring the might of hosts against him, free will always prevails.

So I walked brazenly down the hallway to the front door even though the whole American ramgoat army tried to block my way.

All the shot they fired at me only tickled, and when one of them blasted me with a bazooka at point blank range as I walked out the front door and into the bright sunlight, it felt like a puff of Christmas breeze.

Meanwhile, alarms were howling all over the base, and tanks and lorries rumbled out from underground garages to block my escape, while soldiers came pouring out of barracks, blasting me from every side with every manner and kind of gun and cannon.

But I paid them no mind and just flew up over the barb wire fence of the compound with shot and ray-blast whizzing all around while bombs were bursting in air to the rockets' red glare.

The soldiers took to wing, too, and several of them flew by my side and tried to grab me and weigh me down to make me fall, but I kicked this one, and thumped that one, and kung-fued another one, and with all the yelling and screaming and confusion I broke free and flew into a cloud with the militia in hot pursuit.

I was breezing through the heavens and wafting my way to Jamaica while the ramgoat American Air Force divebombed me and blasted me with all manner of weaponry when God flew out of a cloud and hovered at my side.

"You see what You get me into?" I bawled, ducking as a shell spun past my head and exploded nearby with a tremendous concussion. "Why You fly 'way and leave me?"

God said He felt like a bedtime snack on a nova and He knew I was safe.

"You make de soldiers think I, Taddeus Baps, is a ole negar," I grumbled. "Even me parson migrate. You really ask a lot from a friend, You know."

Meanwhile the heavens around us were exploding with munitions. A jet screeched out of a cloud and blasted us with another ray-shot that just bounced off and fluttered like a misty fishnet towards the earth.

Of course, the weapons couldn't harm God, but I was blown to smithereens several times over Wyoming and Nebraska as we travelled southward, and each time after the direct hit from a missile that splattered me all over creation, I reassembled and God flew to my side chuckling to ask if I liked that or if I wanted a shield, but

I said if He didn't mind I'd rather enjoy the festive blasting since I was still on holiday.

When it was obvious that neither shells nor rays could hurt us, the gunners below began lobbing live sheep at us, hoping to knock us out of the sky with sheep-shot.

Rams and ewes shot out of cannon screamed past our heads, baaing like mad, but as fast as they went up, they tumbled back down to earth wailing and shrieking in tongues, for pampered American sheep is not used to being live ammunition. I watched some of the sheep fall and splatter on the ground, reassemble and try to scamper away, but soldiers chased and grabbed them for ramrodding back into the muzzles of the guns.

We flew over Alabama and Georgia, with sheep-shot spinning and ripping through the air all around us, baaing hideously. But of course, all the sheep-shot in the world was useless, and not a one of them hit God.

Over Georgia I took a couple direct hits from sheep-shot but they only knocked me in a loop for a second and made me feel sweet.

So we made our way out to the Caribbean sea. The soldiers eventually gave up their pursuit and we flew in peace towards Jamaica, where God changed me back into Baps and I resumed my position as shopkeeper in the heavenly village, having experienced the broadening of knowledge that comes with foreign travel.

Later, God remarked casually that His experiment proved that I was wrong and that there was good, too, in the heart of ole negar.

He didn't rub my nose in it, for He is God, and God does not rub nose.

However, I didn't answer Him out of friendship and respect. I just let it drop. Sometimes we Jamaicans just can't explain to foreigners what we know and how we feel, and we're better off just shutting up than even trying. Let the foreigner buy property and plant some cocoa and he'll soon find out for himself about ole negar heart. In fact, I was going to suggest to God that He buy three acres of land that I own in Portland, but I bit my tongue and said sharply to meself, "Hi, Baps! Dis is you friend! You want ole negar thief out Him one crop? Dat is how you treat you friend?"

So I just shut up me mouth and said nothing.

Personally, if it was me reading this book, I'd demand my money back.

Chapter 22

I have a lot of criticisms against this world. I don't say I hate it, but I can't truthfully say that I love it, either. The world does not have to be a place of such woe and tribulation, and it does not have to be the stamping ground of rampant hypocrisy and wholesale shenanigans. I think better is possible. Mankind can be better. Manners and morals can be put on a higher plane. All creatures and things in this world can benefit from improvement.

One day after we'd returned from America, me and God went swimming in a river. As we were drying out on the bank in the sun, the subject of the creation came up and I mentioned my opinions about the world.

I didn't put my point harshly, I just told Him in a kindly way what I have already said—that better was possible.

Baps, God said, Would you like to try your hand at creation?

I lay on the bank for a few moments and thought before I finally said, "Listen God, dis is like two of us playing cricket, with You at bat hitting one run here and one run dere. Now, if I come to bat and on my first stroke I hit a six, how You going feel 'bout it?"

I'll feel good for you, Baps.

"Dat's what You say now. But when my six fly over de boundary, You bound to feel downhearted."

So you think you could do better?

"God! Look! Who is You friend? Who walk and run wid You up here everyday? Who take God-shot from de American ramgoat army meant for You? Who lick down

Harvard anthropology students when dem stone You in de tree?"

Love pulsed out from God as He caressed my headback with His light. I squirmed and patted His light.

"All right, God. Remember, we is two man. People will talk."

God chuckled and said He didn't care what people said, He loved me.

"Lawd God, God! Man not supposed to say dat to man, You know!"

God laughed.

After a few moments, I squirmed and gruffly whispered, "And I love You, too, God. Now, make us drop it. You never know which blackmailing ear listening from behind a bush."

All right, Baps, God said in a disappointed voice. But I wanted to give you a hug.

I sighed and lay quietly on the bank for a minute or two and wondered to myself what I was going to do with a God who didn't realise that man and man not supposed to hug up in private much less in public.

But after a minute's thought, I jumped up and said, "Back foot and crosses, God! Gimme de blasted hug. I don't business who de rass see it!"

And me and God hugged up on the riverbank, His light settling over me like a shimmering web. Then laughing with joy, we scampered back into the water for a refreshing swim.

God would not get off the creation business. He kept nagging me to try my hand at it, to show what I could do that was better, and although I kept putting Him off with a joke, I began staying up at night in the back room of my shop, writing down my ideas for a better world in an exercise book.

This was hard work. The world is not as easy to create as it looks. But I had in mind certain improvements I would immediately make in my creation.

First and foremost, I would create a fart-free woman. I don't care what anybody say, a farting woman is a hardship on creation.

On the other hand, I didn't want to deprive woman of a luscious looking part she needs for wriggling up on the street and in a dancehall. So my improved woman that I drew up in an exercise book had a fat batty for wiggling, but one that discharged no fart.

I had other improvements in mind as well.

Knowing that in Jamaica praedial larceny is a serious problem which is discouraging farmers from planting crops, I designed a mango with a hidden mouth under its peel that, if a thiefing hand touched it, would bawl, "Lemme go, bwoy! I belong to farmer John!" or whatever the name of the said owner of the tree, and if the wretch persisted, the mango would bite the brute on the lip and hold onto him like a bad dog until a district constable could make the arrest.

Banana would likewise bite all praedial larceny thief as would pawpaw and orange. (I also designed a sweetsop that was armed with a hidden machete to chop the tongue of all thief as he opened his mouth to take illegal and unauthorised bite, but I knew that God would object to the violence.)

Some of my other ideas were likewise better than the present stale state of affairs.

For example, because God's design conceals pumpum and hood in the hide-out of crotch, the slack situation has developed where parson can rant and rave about unrighteous woman while his own hood is stiff in the pulpit.

This is, to my mind, unsatisfactory.

I rectified matters by mounting hood and pumpum on man and woman's forehead so that when parson lusted for a sister in the choir, the whole world saw and knew just by glancing at his head front. When a sister sat in a pew pretending to be Biblical while she secretly craved to grind a parson, worshippers would see illegal juice dripping down her cheek. Everyone would know exactly who was out to grind who, making hypocrisy impossible.

One evening Hector, who was now helping me out in the shop, stopped by and I showed him my notes and plans after supper.

"Missah Baps," he objected, rubbing his chin, "is worries you know, sah, to mount hood on a man forehead in full and public view. Dere is wisdom behind crotch and zipper."

"What wisdom?"

"To hide hood from woman, so she don't know what she getting until it unwrap. If it wasn't for dat, whole heap o' man would never get a grind. Woman would grind only de one with de big hood on him head front."

"So I'll make all hood one size."

"Missah Baps! You don't understand woman, sah! Woman don't want socialistic hood. She prefer capitalistic surprise, where she don't know whether she getting a plantain or a Vienna sausage until she peel a crotch. You can't change up de whole world just because parson love to grind church sister on de quiet!"

And God had objections, too, when I showed Him my design.

He asked how I expected people to weewee if I put their private parts on their forehead?

"Duck down dem head inna de toilet bowl. Teach dem humility."

He said, I didn't understand. Where would He put kidney and bladder?

"Dat is a detail. Put dem where dey belong."

He said He couldn't, because weewee didn't flow uphill, and if we put hood on a man's head, we'd have to put his bladder in his brain. And if we did that, where would we put his brain?

"Where de bladder is?"

Baps, God said patiently, Brain is bigger than bladder.

"God, some bladder bigger than some brain. For instance," I started to add, "I know plenty ole ne....," but I caught myself in time and hushed up my mouth.

God said he couldn't put a brain inside a belly. He'd have to make a spine that twisted like a hook to connect to the brain. Furthermore, he added, if He put hood on head and bladder inside the brain, where would He park the kidneys?

"Why You must trouble me with technicality, eh?"

Baps, there's physical law, God said. Physical law must be obeyed.

"All right, den! So put hood back in de crotch. Foster hypocrisy! Encourage holier-than-thou behaviour and indiscipline! I give You a drawing dat is a definite improvement and You turn it down. Don't blame me when You whole world mash up."

I don't blame you, Baps. I'm just saying you can't make a man who weewee from his head and think with his belly.

"I don't want hear no more technicality!" I bawled, getting vexed and walking off in a huff.

Baps, God called after me, you expect me to put a jawbone and teeth on a mango? Where on the mango, Baps? And how will the mango know who to bite? Without a brain for that, Baps, mango will bite even its own owner!

Chapter 23

Everybody who knows me knows that I am not a shirker or a slacker, that I have a good brain and a sound head for business, that I don't gripe over every little trouble, and that when I make up my mind to pursue a goal, I never fail to achieve it. That is the way I was raised—to always do my best and to work hard at realising my ambitions.

So it is not easy for me to admit that as a creator I was a flop.

Of course, I didn't flop because my designs were faulty or my overall plan for the world was not first rate. To this day, I believe that hood and pumpum belong on people's foreheads, and I don't business what God says, I still maintain that a biting mango is an improvement over the present wishy-washy fruit that permits every thiefing mouth to eat it.

And I still believe that if God had suspended physical law, which He said He could not, and allowed me to create people from scratch, my world would have turned out better than His earth.

I did get God to make one man with his hood on his forehead, but the poor fellow was obviously not happy with his private parts being hung in public, and as soon as he could draw breath and walk, he hung a doily over his face to hide his hood and said several prayers to me, Baps, begging to have his hood relocated to a more private spot, claiming that bowing down to a toilet gave him a complex.

Sometime after my creation experiment was over, I met him in heaven where he was working as a cultivator on a small farm in St. Elizabeth, and he attacked me with a machete, shrieking, "Put me hood on me headfront and make me look like a rhinoceros, you rass dog you!"

He gave me at least fifty chops, all of which I thoroughly enjoyed, and when he saw that I was relishing his attack, he abruptly stopped it and stormed away grumbling that if he ever met me up on earth in mortal form, he would cut my throat and shove me headfirst down a toilet so I could personally experience the indignity of forehead weeweeing.

"You have to admit dat you were not a hypocrite!" I called after him, as he stormed away.

"How could I be a hypocrite?" he shrieked, beside himself. "I couldn't even see to walk with me blasted hood drape over me eye!"

One evening me and God flew to a distant dark corner of the universe that was bare of planet and wrapped in night and looked like the kind of hill-and-gully place where celestial cobweb might lurk. God had just nyamed out five novas in the Milky Way, and He was feeling powerful and strong.

All right, Baps, He said. Create a better world.

He created a world as I instructed, and I reigned over it for an aeon. Of course, an aeon to God is not even a flea bite, for time does not exist in His presence, and it all went past in a blink.

I don't know exactly where God got the people from to put into my world, for that was His business, not mine. I was only interested in ruling over them, no matter if they came from Timbuktu.

It was a world that looked like the one we presently walk on—round and adorned with hills, valleys, rivers, streams, and oceans—and it was shaped that way not because I especially wanted it, but because of physical law, which God said He could not ignore.

My personal preference was for a flat world where a family could go for a Sunday drive to the edge and peer into space, but God said that gravity would not support a flat earth so we had to settle for the typical fool-fool ball spinning through the fluxy heavens like a gig.

Since God would not let me change the form of man and execute the improvements I have already discussed, He made the inhabitants of my world to look much like you and me with this exception: they had no free will. I also instructed God to make them so that they would know that I, Baps, was their God, so that there was no other God but Baps, so that there would be no doubt in their minds about who Baps was or whether or not they should bow down to Baps, so that they would never question my authority or ponder about my nature, so that when I said 'Jump!' every bitch one of them must jump without argument, and He said, All right, Baps, and did maketh my man and woman according to these specifications.

I ruled over them for one hundred years.

I would appear unto them and walk among them and they would fall prostrate on their faces and wail, "Almighty Baps! You are our Lord and God!"

And to prove it, I instituted a ritual where they would kiss my batty during worship.

And every blessed one of them, from elder to juvenile, worshipped as they were ordered by their creator and kissed my batty whenever I walked among them.

One time I remember as one old woman was getting ready to fervently kiss my batty, I said unto her,

"Woman, talk de truth! Wouldst thou rather not bite Baps' batty?"

"No, Baps!" she cried with horror. "I could never bite thy batty. Thou art God and I love thee."

And the whole lot of them continued to love me for one hundred years, no matter what trouble and woe I visited upon them, for they had no free will.

Sometimes a cranky spirit came over me to clap the wretches with a thunderbolt and blow a few of them to smithereens—to test their love and devotion—and without fail, even after their wives and husbands and children were blasted to pieces before their very eyes, verily, they would come rushing up to me to kiss said batty in devout worship, and when I wouldst tempt them and say, "Now, talk de truth! I just dynamited thy family to Kingdom come! Wouldst thou rather not bite my holy batty than kiss it?" the multitude would wail and rend their garments and gnash their teeth and pop oath that they would rather kiss Baps' batty for worship and never wouldst bite it no matter how Baps might smite them.

After one hundred years of ruling over them, I grew weary of the nasty batty-kissing brutes.

"Dis is no fun," I complained to God. "Dem come just like robots."

God said, Yea, Baps, that's the problem with creating people without free will.

"All right! So, give dem a free will."

God said if that was my desire He would comply, but with that came free choice, and with free choice must come random.

"What?"

Things will happen on their own, some good, some bad. And you Baps will have no control over events.

"You mean to say dat a wicked man might live long and prosper and dead in him sleep while a good hardworking man might get lick down by a bus in de flower of youth?"

Exactly.

"Dat is how Your world run now! I want a better world dan Yours! Me not dealing wid no random!"

Baps, you can't have free will without free choice. If you have choice, it means that nothing can be foreseen or preplanned.

"So according to You, under random a good man could prosper and live a long, happy, fruitful life and die in him sleep with contentment and glory?"

Yes.

"Name one such man," I dared Him.

Baps, I don't get into particular cases. That is not my affair.

"You are God! It supposed to be Your affair!"

If I make it my affair, it won't be random.

I suffered a long pause to pass between us, for verily, I was well vexed with this unrighteous state of affairs.

"All right, God," I finally said. "I will agree dat random can rule my world. But I need a hell to cleanse de wicked with fire."

Certainly, Baps. If that's what you wish.

He had given in so easily that I got suspicious.

"Hold on, now! In my hell, de fire must really burn and make sinners howl with pain."

God grew silent and saith nothing for a long while, which I found out later was the passing of twenty years.

No, Baps, He finally saith. I can't change the laws of heaven. You know law number two is Thou shalt feel good no matter what.

I was upseteth and it showeth plenty, for I paceth up and down in the gardens of my world and gnasheth my teeth as I tried to comprehend the reasoning behind God's bullheadedness.

Finally, overwrought, I went up to God and we had it out on the spot.

"God," I told Him, "I am a reasonable man."

Verily, Baps.

"Now, tell me plainly. Why can't I have a hell to burn a few sinners for a little bit? I don't want to burn dem for eternity like de Americans. Dat is too patriotic. How about a ten thousand year hell? You give me a hell with real fire and real pain, and I get to broil my sinners in it for ten thousand years. By den dem well cook up, anyway. Wha' you say?"

One hundred years passed.

And God said No.

"Why?" I asked, kicking a nearby bush in my vexation.

God grew silent for another hundred years.

And God trembled and wept.

I rushed quickly to His side and embraced His light and comforteth Him, and the light of God sobbed in my arms.

"God!" I bawled, giving His light a little shake. "Why dost Thou weep?"

Because, Baps, saith God, I can't stand pain.

"You can't stand pain? Who giving You pain? I'll thump down his rass on de spot!"

You want to give me pain, Baps.

"Me?! Me, poor poor sinner give You, God Almighty, me best friend in de universe, pain? Bite You tongue, God! Shame on You!"

God said He hath not a tongue to biteth.

"Well, bite anything! For I would never give You pain. Is sinners I want to burn, not You! You know dat!"

But Baps, saith God, I am the sinners.

"How You mean? You're de nicest man in de world. You couldn't even mash a ant!"

Baps, saith God, all things are me, and I am all things. If thou burnest a sinner to suffer real pain, thou burnest me. I hateth the pain of fire, Baps. Don't burnest me.

"So dat's why You have nothing but sweetness and joy up here, for if real pain was up here, You'd feel it, too?"

Thou saith it, Baps. And I hateth pain.

"But how come You don't feel de pain from earth?"

I do, but my small size and the large distance giveth me merciful and needful buffer. However, every now and again I feel a pinprick.

I paceth my world, carrying God in my arms, while I contemplated His truth.

I walked my world for twenty, nay, thirty circumferences. Then I declared unto God, "God, Thou art too softhearted. You need to come down to earth and keep shop with me sometime and mix up with Jamaican ole negar. Dey will toughen You up."

I don't think so, Baps. Ole negar is me, too.

So I gave up on hell and told God that He could give my created subjects free will and loosen random upon them.

And over these wretches I reigned another hundred years as God.

Under this kingdom of random, all manner of wickedness and viciousness spread among my people. Evildoers prospered; pious men and women drowned or on their way to Sunday service suffered unprovoked bucking down in fields by unruly bulls. Innocent children choked on their food, while vicious liars prospered and grew fat. Plotting, scheming, and backbiting ran amok among the population. Disease struck down the virtuous and the wicked in equal parts. Driveby shooting developed in the city parts; goat grinding spread among the country youth.

I had told God that I wanted my world to be simple, that my people could keep a goat or a sheep but were barred from any mechanical invention such as weapons, slingshot, spear, and bow and arrow; that they might keepeth a crookstick and eateth harddough bread and bun and cheese and yam and ackee and saltfish—a hardy fare for a simple life—and God said, Yea Baps, but with random the simple life might not last long, and I said, You leave that to me, I'll show You how to manage a world.

And at first, I checked progress and stemmed wickedness, for as soon as I spotted a wrongdoer, I'd appear unto him or her and bellow, "Ye rass, ye! I saw dat! Take dis, dirty brute!" and blast the wretch with lightning, sending him straight to heaven.

Then one day I was struck by horrible betrayal and blasphemous doublecross that taught me a lesson.

I was flying over my creation when I spotted a man and a woman arguing on a country trail, and even as I watched the man picketh up a rockstone and busteth open the woman's head. She fell onto the ground, wallowing and bleeding while the man scrambled for another rockstone, but I appeared unto him and said, "You want bust something, bust dis!" and blasted him with a thunderbolt.

The woman got off the ground, holding her bleeding head, and stood mutely looking down at the smoking charcoal heap that remained of her assailant and then, approaching, she declared her wish to kiss my Godly batty.

I consented to permit grateful worship and she stooped down and tore a big chunk out of the right cheek of said batty with a vicious bulldog bite.

Now even though the bite felt sweet, for I was still under heavenly conditions, I bawled, "Rass, woman! Thou bitest batty! Ungrateful wretch! Why?"

"To teach you to keep you damn nose out of my blasted business!" she growled, charging me like a wild beast as if to chunk out flesh from the left cheek, and she wore such a snarling ferocity that I flew up in a tree and pitched on a limb while she roamed beneath, circling the trunk and stoning me as if I were a lowly pea dove.

"I don't understand dese people," I grumbled later to God, telling Him about the incident.

God said, Baps, you haven't seen anything yet.

"You and You random mash dem up. Dere mentality is too rebellious and contrary. You can't trust dem."

That's because they have free will, said God.

"Free will or no free will, nobody biting my batty again," I groused. "From henceforth, all batty kissing is banned from worship service. Make de brutes build temple and burn incense. Days of batty kissing worship done."

God said solemnly that He thought that was a good idea.

"You like a fatted calf," I mumbled defensively, "I like a batty kiss."

My populace grew fierce, undisciplined and unruly. As soon as I smote one for a wickedness, another took his place and committeth an even greater wickedness. I fleweth about my world here and there smiting and clapping on headside and headback with thunderbolt to maintain discipline, civility and righteousness, but with the people engaged in rampant grinding, they bred like flies and multiplied, formeth sects and cults, held up Baals before me, denied my divinity, and when I would intervene and singe their rass, they would say afterwards that I was not a God but UFO or Bigfoot; that I was earthquake and hurricane and other worldly disturbance; and when I appeared unto their doubting scholars and scribes and declared, "It is I! God Baps!" they would say, "If thou art Baps, submit to analysis and probe," and when I would bellow indignantly, "Probe where? What you want to probe? Thou shalt not probe the Lord thy God!" they would smirketh among themselves and whisper, "This is the bad roast beef we ate for dinner that has travelled to our brains and now giveth us hallucination. This is no God!" and if I caused a thunderbolt to explode among them, they would whimper, "Verily, the gravy was rancid, too!"

They invented weapons, fought wars, slaughtered nations, committed atrocities, and it became an endless and backbreaking labour to fly around and smite unrighteousness, stem rumour-mongering, curb praedial larceny and blasphemy, reign in backbiting, and quell sinfulness.

Random travelled among them, maiming and killing the blessed and the gentle as well as the rough-shod and the wicked, and a mighty wailing of voices swelled out from my earth, crying that there was no justice, no order, that Baps was gunman, brute, pettifogger and wretch. False prophets wandered my earth proclaiming themselves the one and only true Baps, and people gathered around them and kissed their batty instead of mine, and I was so sorely vexed at this that after attending a revival meeting and blasting two evangelist before the congregation who screamed at me and called me 'dirty Bigfoot,' I withdrew to the backwoods and brooded among sinless rockstones.

And I was sitting brooding in a clearing when I met a righteous shepherd, a mild young man who spaketh good English and showeth nice manners and wore freshly pressed clothing, and he bowed down and hailed me as Baps, and he gave me no back talk, no indiscipline, no argument, and I was so pleased with his behaviour that I smote him with a thunderbolt and sent him straight to heaven.

But as I sat alone among the unthinking rockstone with charcoal smouldering at my feet that had once been a well-mannered shepherd, I was so mystified by what I had done that I bawled unto God for explanation and He appeared unto me.

"God," I said, "I am a wretch and a beast!"

What did you do now?

"I just blasted a decent young man of good upbringing and manners and sent him to heaven. See where de spot o' ground singe? Dat was him."

God said, Yea, Baps, I saw him entering heaven, singing your praise.

"But, God!" I protested. "A few minutes earlier I smote a thiefing evangelist in a revival tent."

Yea Baps, and he, too, has reached heaven. But he praises you not.

"You don't understand, God," I groused, "I licked one down 'cause him bad and I lick anodder one down 'cause him good. And two of dem gone to cock up dem foot in de same heaven."

169

Yea, Baps.

"And I just see a serious problem wid Your world now. And it is dis: How You expect people to get better?"

God said, They must get better on their own, Baps.

"Hah! Without fire and brimstone?"

Yea, Baps. And better that springs from the heart is always better than better that comes from fear of fire.

I studied the face of God for a hundred years before I replied, "God, You more subtle than a Chinyman," and as I impulsively got down on bended knee to worship Him God squawked, Hey, Baps! No bother with no batty kissing!

I laughed and at that moment I gave up my creation, for I saw that God's brain was filled with wisdom while mine own had been ruined over the years of coping with pettifogging earthly woe.

God devoured my short-term world in this far-flung corner of the universe and we journeyed back to heaven's Jamaica.

Chapter 24

When I returned to heaven, I suffered hardship and abuse over my experiment as a creator. What God had done—I don't know how, as I said, and I never asked Him—was borrow some souls from heaven to use in my creation experiment. But ole negar does not like to be used as guinea pig even if the result is advancement in understanding of otherworldly philosophy, and whenever I bucked up any of my former subjects on the streets of heaven, they would cuss me out royally.

Some cussed me for making them bow down when I was their God. Several ranted and raved at me for making them kiss my batty in worship. Others complained that I had been a shoddy and good-for-nothing God, no better than a ragamuffin idol. One woman alleged that my slipshod reign as God only proved that negar man should never mount the heavenly throne, while another screamed in my ears that mine was the nastiest tasting batty she had ever had to kiss, and she well knew 'bout batty kissing for on earth she had been a politician.

A few licked me down or chopped me up in the street, and the most vicious among them simply growled at me as I walked past, "I won't give you de pleasure of a blow."

The woman whose attacker I had blasted with a thunderbolt, getting a severe batty bite for all my trouble, paid me back by giving me fifty-five grind one night to show that I had been a worthless and good-for-nothing God. She left telling me that she would come back the next day and grind me until my eyeball fell out.

But she never came back—out of pure spite.

My attempt at creation was the last big adventure me and God shared.

True, we went on a few small jaunts to Japan and Korea, and one time we travelled to France to see the opening of a Parisian PlayHell that offered the public affordable family broiling in hellfire. We strolled the catwalks lining the various chambers of this hell and chuckled as we watched French children plunge into the fiery pits, splashing joyfully and shrieking, "Papa! Mama! Ooo La La!" Parisians patiently waited hours in line for the chance to spend a restful Sunday afternoon skylarking among fire and brimstone.

"What a place, eh, God?" I marvelled as we leaned over the railing of the catwalk and ogled the revellers.

Look at that child! God laughed, pointing to one spunky boy who was doing a swan dive into a lake of molten fire from a rocky ledge. He plunged into the brimstone and romped to the surface squealing, "Oh, Papa! I want to stay here for eternity!"

When the complex was first opened, the US government immediately issued visa restrictions barring its citizens from travel to France. There was hotheaded talk about a Cuban-style boycott like the Americans had had down on earth against Fidel Castro. Congress angrily threatened bombardment over what it viewed as France's mockery of America's most cherished national ideal.

The French government issued a curt diplomatic statement to the effect that history had shown the Americans to be undependable when it came to promised attacks, that France would observe no festivities in anticipation of any American bombardment, and if one were received, France would gratefully enjoy it but not reciprocate.

Then the row died down.

One morning I got up early, crawled through the culvert, and impulsively paid a visit to earthly Jamaica. I wanted to see what had happened to my holdings since my death, for I had had no children or wife to inherit my worldly goods and had left no will.

I had been meaning to make the journey for some time, but my friendship with God and the wonderful lifestyle of heaven had always stopped me. But this morning I just got it into my head to check out Jamaica in a day trip.

The village was awash in morning mists when I stepped into the streets of heaven, and it was so lovely and peaceful walking down the glistening road that even though I am not an emotional man, I almost felt to cry with joy.

In the shimmering morning fog, the only person waiting on the sloping grassland onto which the culvert emptied was the battleaxe who had licked me down with a rockstone on my arrival.

I told her 'good morning' and asked if her husband had come yet or if she was still waiting. She grumbled that he had been sick and should arrive any minute now, but she suspected that the dirty dog was putting up a fight on his deathbed because of bad conscience.

"When him reach, him know I goin' lick him down," she blared cantankerously, stirring the pile of rockstones at her feet with her shoe and keeping her eye fastened to the mouth of the culvert.

We heard the sound of breeze blowing in the pipe, and the woman quickly grabbed a rockstone and perched herself in a position of ambush.

I saw a soul solidifying out of the culvert, and as soon as he had gelled out of duppy fog and into his solid body shape, she roared, "You stinking brute! You finally reach!" and flung the rockstone point-blank at his head, knocking him viciously onto the grass.

The man fluttered on the ground for a second or two with ecstasy and blinked up groggily at his attacker.

"Daisy? Is you dat? How come you lick so sweet?" he babbled, rubbing his head with joy. "You lick never so sweet on earth."

"You brute, you!" she screamed, hoisting another rockstone. "You grind de widow next door before me even turn cold!"

"Is true," he chuckled, turning his temple to absorb the second blow. "I definitely need a beating!"

She glared at him for a minute before tossing the rockstone aside and grimly barking, "No!"

"Lawd, Daisy!" he blurted. "Is not only de widow I grind, you know! On de evening of you nine-night service, I grind Miss Jessie daughter in de canepiece, too."

"No! No matter what you say! I not licking you again!"

As they were arguing about it, Hopeton curdled onto the slopes of the hillside.

"Miss Daisy!" he grinned, getting up and dusting off. "You husband finally reach!"

"Hopeton, tell her," the man begged, standing up wobbly, "what I was doing when I dead."

"Him was trying to feel up de batty of de hospital matron, Miss Daisy. De excitement kill him."

"You dog! No matter what him or you say, I not licking you again. You want a lick, you shoulda live a good life."

"Lawd, Daisy! No go on so! Bust me head, nuh, man!"

Still quarrelling, they followed Hopeton down the slopes of the hillside, the man trying to taunt his wife into another attack, while she obstinately refused, scolding, "Next time, wait 'til me body cold before you go grind every nasty woman in de parish."

And in the harmonious ending to this dispute, which on earth would have led to murder, court trial, and the gallows, I beheld the wisdom of the Lord.

Chapter 25

What I saw that day in Jamaica aggravated me no end.

My house had been captured by Mabel, my conniving maid, and turned into a tenement for her relatives from the country. Clothes were hanging everywhere over the front yard. Dirty dishes were piled up in the sink. Stinking shoes and socks littered my drawing room. In broad daylight Mabel was catching a morning grind on my own bed with one of the policemen who had investigated my death, the two of them sweating up my good cotton sheets.

I flew to the countryside and found that Mabel and her relatives had likewise captured my businesses. Chaos and indiscipline ruled over my three shops. Goods were misfiled and scattered across the shelves. Rude-boy youths slouched on the premises, and a general atmosphere of disorderliness and rowdyism ran rampant.

It burned me to see all my life's work and hard-earned goods so squandered and abused. Indeed, I was so vexed that even though I flew past a cottage in the country and spotted a church sister lying naked in bed and heard her muttering hopefully that duppy better not come ride her during her afternoon nap, I just glided on to the culvert.

That evening on our walk, God asked me why I was so quiet and I told Him.

"You know how hard I work to keep me shops in good operating order, God," I griped. "You should see what ole negar do to dem."

God asked me what they did.

"God, dey have bully beef shelve beside sardine and salmon! What kind of foolishness is dat?"

God said He had no idea.

"You always shelve beef wid beef, God," I explained, trying not to sound grumpy for I knew that He was inexperienced in shopkeeping. "Bully beef belong beside Vienna sausage and Spam. Not beside sardine! Dat's out of order!"

God said, Oh.

"Sardine belong with herring. And herring belong with salmon. Fish wid fish and beef wid beef. And fish and beef don't sit side by side on de same shelf!"

We walked on some more when God suddenly asked me if I would like to return to Jamaica.

"How?"

It will be as if you never died.

"But would I remember what happened?"

If you want to.

I stopped dead in my tracks. We had come to the clearing where I had tied up the philosopher a long time ago, and I looked hard and deep at God.

"You would do dis for me, God?"

Yes, Baps. You are my best friend.

My head was spinning and my heart was jumping at the prospect, but then I remembered that I would be leaving God behind and I didn't feel good about it, but God told me not to fret for I would be back in a blink, and that me and Him would always be best friend.

I thought for a moment, standing in the clearing that evening as the sunset of heaven splashed a pot of paint across the sky, and I said, "Yes, God. Bully beef don't belong beside sardine on a shelf. I want to go back."

****

God and me travelled the next morning to Jamaica, where He couldn't linger long because the world is a dread chamber of pain for Him.

He hurried me to my house and took me back in time to the moment when I had died that Saturday morning. He had spent the night before nyaming out a few constellations, so He was well bright and powerful.

We hugged up in my drawing room as we hovered over my body, God wincing from the worldwide chopping, shooting, thumping, burning, thiefing, drowning, murdering, shoplifting, slandering, embezzling, raping—all the hourly woe, anguish, and tragedy on the face of this dirty earth—but trying His best not to show His pain. He told me to lie on the floor beside my dead body.

"God," I said, as I lay down on the floor, "do You mind if I write a book about me days in heaven?"

God said, No, He didn't mind one bit.

"Any deep message You want me to put in?"

God said, yes. We should stop all the fool-fool preaching against tomtom....

"Is 'pumpum' not 'tomtom'."

Whatever. Stop all the fretting about it and be kind and loving to one another.

"How You can call 'pumpum' 'tomtom'? What's de matter wid You, eh, God?"

I have to go, Baps.

"I need a deeper message dan dat."

That's my message, Baps.

"I need something wid Biblical word in it, man!" I grumbled. "Say something with 'shalt' or 'thou' or something deep."

178

But God said He had never been deep. It was mankind who was deep.

And wincing from the million wounds and cruelties being inflicted every second all over this nasty globe, His light gave me a gentle kiss on the cheek, and God Almighty disappeared.

Chapter 26

The next thing I remember was the sound of Mabel bawling out my name, "Mr. Baps! Mr. Baps!" and this time when she peeped cautiously into the drawing room and was about to shriek that I was dead, I jumped up from the floor like I had fallen and calmly dusted myself off.

"Wha' happen, Missah Baps?" she stammered, peering suspiciously at me in the dim morning light.

"I fall off de hassock," I said gruffly.

"Oh."

"Beg you a cup o' morning tea."

"Yes, sah."

She flopped away in her loose-fitting slippers.

When she returned I was standing by the window breathing the dawn breeze of my second life and planning my first day back on earth. She put the tea on a table and was leaving when I called out to her, "Mabel, remember de little pumpum I was begging you?"

She stood warily in the doorway, her face set in the cautious expression of a pedestrian approaching a snarling dog in the street. "Yes, sah."

"Well, I want you to know dat I don't want it again."

"Yes, sah?"

"No. And it won't affect you job, either. You have a job wid me as long as you do de work. I change me ways."

She shuffled hesitantly in the doorway and peered at her feet.

"I was goin' give you tonight, Missah Baps," she finally said in a downhearted voice.

"Well, you don't have to."

"But I was goin' give you, sah."

"Mabel, I say you don't have to!"

"But I still was goin' give you anyway, sah."

I saw at once that she was upset, confused, and afraid that I was playing a malicious trick on her. I said to myself, "Baps, you should take de pumpum, you know, under dese circumstances. Dis is not heaven, where pumpum plentiful and abundant and no man walks without. Dis is mangy, dirty-minded earth where pumpum is scarce, under Biblical curse, and tough to find. You should take it, man, and make de poor chile feel better 'bout her prospects in life. You should take it, for while you were dead, she paid herself deceitful Leap Year bonus, thiefed you house and captured you shops. She use you head as her footstool. She grind policeman on you bed. She file bully beef next to herring."

But in the next breath I thought, yes, she is a wicked woman, but I am not a *shouldist* whose brain is ruled by empty-headed *should*. My duppy hath abided in heaven and has known truth. Verily, Baps, renounce all pumpum tendered under compulsion and pressure.

So I saith unto her, "Mabel, talk de truth. If I say no, I don't want it, would you feel worthless and good-for-nothing, like life not worth living?"

She hung her head and muttered in a small voice, "Yes, sah."

But I could tell from the quiver in her lip that she spake a lie. So I said to her, "Well, Mabel, I'm sorry to make you feel bad, but I have changed me ways. I don't want it."

She brightened visibly, as if she'd suddenly seen that the snarling dog was chained up.

"Well, if you change you mind, Missah Baps, come to me room 'bout eight o'clock," she sniffed, bounding through the door and hurrying away from the dog.

And I must admit that it burned my rass to see her leave.

It burneth my rass bad, bad.

And when eight o'clock came, it burneth my rass something wicked.

But I got thick rope, lashed myself to the bedpost and remained steadfastly in my room until the invited hour had passed.

I had just returned from heaven.

And verily Baps had forever changed his ways.

I have tried, since my return to earthly Jamaica, to live in such a way that God will never ever feel a pinprick of pain from my any word or deed. I have tried to explain truth to various shortsighted people around me like Hector, my old gardener, who I knew was not long for this world.

One morning I attempted to instruct him in the higher road by asking him what he would do if he suddenly journeyed to a land where he could get a new hood or a new brain or both.

He gaped at me as if I'd gone mad. "New hood or brain, sah?"

"Or both."

"Me would take de new brain, sah," he lied.

"Do dat, Hector! Or take both! Don't just take new hood."

Later as I walked past the kitchen I overheard him whispering to Mabel, "Missah Baps going off him head."

A year later he fell out of the mango tree in the backyard and broke his neck, and while Mabel was shrieking her head off at the sight of his dead body twisted at the root of the tree, I stooped down and whispered to Hector to look around for Hopeton, to go with him on the minibus and into the culvert, and when he got to heaven to choose not only hood, but also brain.

I can well imagine how confused and afraid he must have been to float out of his broken body, hear Mabel's frantic screaming, and listen to me telling him about Hopeton and choosing while he gazed around the backyard wondering what in the world was happening.

"Go peacefully into de culvert, Hector," I urged him as Mabel's hysterical wailing pealed through the backyard and deafened my ears. "You have more to fear from man than from God. And where you are going, neither God nor man will hurt you."

ABOUT THE AUTHOR

Anthony C. Winkler was born in Kingston, Jamaica. He was educated at Mount Alvernia Academy then Cornwall College in Montego Bay, and California State University in Los Angeles. He is the author of several textbooks in English and Public Speaking which are widely used in American colleges and universities.

His first novel, The Painted Canoe, *was published by Kingston Publishers in 1983, followed by* The Lunatic *in 1987 and* The Great Yacht Race *in 1992. American editions of the first two novels were published by Lyle Stuart in 1986 and 1987 respectively. All three novels met with international critical acclaim, and the movie* The Lunatic *was released in 1990.* Going Home to Teach, *an autobiographical account of a year spent in Jamaica, was published in 1995.*

Mr Winkler currently lives in Atlanta, Georgia, with his wife and two children.